PARADISE ALLEY

SYLVESTER STALLONE

PARADISE ALLEY

ILLUSTRATIONS BY TOM WRIGHT

G.P. PUTNAM'S SONS · NEW YORK

SBN: 399-12080-7

Library of Congress Cataloging in Publication Data

Stallone, Sylvester.
Paradise Alley.

I. Title.
PZ4.S78334He [PS3569.T3214] 813'.5'4 77-22926

PRINTED IN THE UNITED STATES OF AMERICA

TO SASHA,

WHO TAKES AWAY THE RAIN

PARADISE ALLEY

1

HELL'S KITCHEN, NEW YORK, WAS PROBA-
bly the hottest place on earth during the summer of '46.

No one really felt like moving during the summer of
'46. Old people with wrinkled skin and gray hair that
stuck to the nape of their sweaty necks leaned from the
tenement windows like wilted flowers and tried to fan
themselves. It was not worth it because it took too much
effort and it did no good. Above these wilted humans
hung a maze of clothes lines that sagged and wove a
pattern five stories above the streets, and on a good wash
day nearly blotted out the sun. If Hell's Kitchen ever
decided to have a national flag, it most likely would be a
pair of yellow-stained boxer shorts flapping from a frayed
clothes line.

A dilapidated ice truck crept around the corner of 46th
Street, and angled up Ninth Avenue, and tar-spotted

children ran after the truck and scooped their hands to capture the cool water that trickled from the rear.

It was like magic how the handkerchiefs and filthy tissues now fluttered in people's hands begging the iceman for help.

People screamed for ice.

People threatened for ice.

Some tarts even offered their curves for ice.

During the winter God was the most important thing to the poor slobs of Hell's Kitchen, but during the summer, ice was God.

Victor Carboni had been driving an ice truck since, well who could remember, and now he was twenty-eight. As usual, Victor would drive along sucking on a piece of ice, and patting his dog, Bella, who was wound like an old rag around the bent floor shift that grew out of the truck's belly.

Victor Carboni had a pile of dark hair that was never combed.

He was very tall, and possessed rare strength, and when people would watch Victor hauling huge blocks of ice from the back of his truck, they would say that the young Italian had been born an ox.

Not true.

Victor had become an ox through hard toil. Some people have hobbies that are for relaxing. Victor's hobby was sweat and work—it's what he liked best, but more important, it's what he understood. And it was strange that Victor always felt strongest early in the morning. It was common fact around the neighborhood that on a good morning Victor could haul over 450 pounds up five flights of steps without blowing his breakfast.

No other iceman in New York could do that.

No other iceman in New York would want to.

"Victor! You sonofabitch! Gimme ice! Gimme ice!"

"Not today, Mr. Locco, ya not on the list."

"Gimme ice!"

Victor smiled at the cursing. He was used to it and considered it part of the business.

Nothing bothered Victor.

Once a man, insane from the heat, threatened him with a large German gun for ice, and Victor was slightly scared, and when he was scared he would laugh, and Victor laughed so hard at the gunman running alongside the truck, he nearly drove the machine into a group of fruit vendors gathered around a dog who had just keeled over from a heat stroke.

Nothing bothered Victor.

"Sorry— you get ice tomorrow, Mr. Locco. Today is not your day!" Victor yelled.

Victor rang the bell a few more times and tossed pieces of cracked ice at the little dirty hands that reached out to his moving ice truck.

Victor saw a few children who were not running after the truck but stayed on the sidewalk touching something dead with a stick. It was another mutt dog who had just decided to die from the heat.

A lady with a pitted face yelled from a third story

window, "Push it away! It's gonna rot! Push it with your foot!"

"Push it with ya nose!" a brat shot back.

"I'm callin' the cops!"

"Ya ain't gotta telephone, ugly," another brat said and laughed.

"What happened?" Victor said and leaned from the truck.

"The heat killed 'im."

" . . . Why don't you guys take 'im to the river?" Victor said and leaned back inside.

The kids started to move the hairy corpse down the street with their feet and Victor pulled away.

Victor was not the smartest guy in Hell's Kitchen.

Not the best looking.

But one thing was for sure.

Victor the iceman was a rolling neighborhood institution.

2

THE DRIPPING TRUCK ROCKED DOWN
Eighth Avenue and Victor could not help feeling good.

He was young, he was strong, maybe not too bright,
but he was a happy person. It is as though the Lord had
purposely shoved him into the ice house and said, "This
is it, Vic." Victor enjoyed his job, and though he never
said it, he would do it for free. Since he made only forty
cents an hour, he almost did.

On the outskirts of Hell's Kitchen a young soldier who
had no legs and was blind sat propped upon a peach
crate. The soldier and the crate were set up on the
corner of 49th and Eighth. Though badly crippled, the
soldier seemed to have an almost nauseating amount of
patriotic energy in his gut. There he sat with a helmet
wedged between his stumps and a cardboard sign hanging from a string around his neck. On the sign, scrawled

in crayon, was "GOD BLESS FREEDOM!" Whenever the blind veteran heard people approach, he would automatically begin to moan the song, "Over There." He never failed to at least get two bits an hour, and the more change that was dropped in his helmet the louder he moaned "Over There."

God knows if someone had ever dropped a dollar bill into his helmet he most likely would have fallen off his crate and broken into a criminally sour aria . . . A pigeon landed on a building overhang . . . It crapped on the vet and flew away. The bird wasn't a music lover.

Victor saw the soldier a half a block away as he veered to the curb in front of Schwartz' grocery store. Victor stroked his dog, then leaped out of the truck, but upon landing, his large face turned red. He did not hear the usual sound of his leather heel landing against cement. Victor looked down at the still warm mound of dog waste that was pancaked beneath his shoe and splattered against his white socks. He glanced around to see if anyone was laughing at his dilemma, and no one was, whereupon he began to drag his heel along the curb until he felt his shoe was once again back to its normal odor.

He had dragged his foot nearly a block before he was satisfied, and striding back to the ice truck, snatched up 200 pounds with a pair of iron tongs, and entered Schwartz'.

Mr. Schwartz stopped yelling at his wife when he heard the bell to his front door and saw the broad shoulders enter.

"Don't buy buttermilk. I can't sell buttermilk— Here comes my favorite iceman."

"How about us going to Coney Island for the day, Mr. Schwartz?"

"Too busy ... When you gettin' married, Victor?"

"When I get rich."

"That's nice."

"Ya need some air, Mr. Schwartz. Old people need air."

"You're givin' me air, Victor."

"I don't want ya gettin' sick."

"Like a horse I am."

Victor stashed the squares of ice in the ice box at the rear of the store and walked back to Mr. Schwartz. Mr. Schwartz held out three Brazil nuts and Victor crushed them in his right hand and returned them to Mr. Schwartz. This was a game they had started three years ago and Mr. Schwartz had never failed to play it every time Victor delivered.

"Goodbye, Victor," Schwartz said and turned to his wife stacking cans. "You—eat these."

When Victor walked out of Mr. Schwartz' grocery store, he looked down the street and studied the soldier propped on the peach crate.

Victor slipped a jaw breaker into his mouth and sort of strolled towards the soldier, trying not to smile. Standing beside the humming soldier, the iceman glanced both ways, bent over and lifted the crate and soldier, and walked halfway up the street and placed them both in the rear of the truck.

"You're getting too heavy," Victor said.

"Just drive, Stupid."

"Gainin' weight?"

"Shut up."

Victor eased behind the wheel, started the truck, stroked his dog again, and put the machine in gear.

The soldier took off his hat, and black hair fell nearly below his ears.

He then peeled off the blindfold and extracted his legs from inside the crate and stretched ... He studied the pigeon crap that stained his uniform and groaned.

The phony soldier was Cosmo Carboni and he was Victor's older brother, and was no masterpiece of kindness.

He had a medium skeleton.

Well, maybe not medium.

But odd.

No, odd is the wrong word:

Cosmo Carboni was an angular piece of hustling machinery bent into the form of a man. His dark eyes resembled a pair of oiled raisins jammed into his skull with a broom handle. His shockingly long hair was shiny enough to reflect the sun, and a thing that resembled a banana was considered his nose. An urban Indian is what he most resembled.

Cosmo may not have been a pin-up, but what this bum had was wit.

He was a gymnast of scams and petty cons, a charmer

with dirty fingernails and had declared himself the most promising human being in the history of Hell's Kitchen. Yes, he was very proud of being a con-man, and proud of using his wits instead of his muscles to earn a living. A long time ago he had figured that anybody who used sweat instead of smarts to get ahead in life has to be a certified jerk. He liked his strong brother, but he also thought Victor was a jerk for working like a dockyard horse when there was easy money to be had.

Easy, that is,

If you were witty.

Cosmo had been sitting with his legs tied in a knot on the peach crate for the past six hours using his wits, and now he was hot, tired and had a brainful of dead humor. The army uniform was like a wool furnace and Cosmo palmed away the sweat that snaked down his forehead. And refused to acknowledge the white spots of pigeon crap a second time.

"Whew! I gotta scrap this gimmick! When a guy can't make peanuts pretending he's a cripple, the world's getting to be a cheap place," Cosmo said, and fished a mangled cigarette butt out of his sock and lit it with a stick match.

"A real cheap place— I'd like to kill every bird in this city!" Cosmo yelled and scared Victor.

As Cosmo bounced down West 47th Street, he viewed his neighborhood with an acid taste in his mouth.

He hated it.

He hated the slobs that were born, lived, bred and died there, and had the nerve to say they had lived a full life.

Their lives had been full all right, full of yesterday's news. He knew one day, with the right break, he could take over this dump neighborhood and do it up with style. He would be famous enough to have the name "Hell's Kitchen" maybe legally changed to "Cosmo's Kitchen."

At the intersection, one ragman was arguing with a taller ragman over territorial rights. The argument was beginning to stop traffic, but the filthy ragmen acted like their business was much more important than anyone else's. The short ragman screamed and kicked the tall ragman's cart.

"Drive around them creeps," Cosmo said and spit.

"I can't drive on the sidewalk!"

"C'mon, get gutsy!"

Cosmo was in no humor to debate with his iceman brother, and yanked the steering wheel and veered onto the sidewalk. The truck angled around the ragmen, and Cosmo leaned across his brother, snatched the short ragman's hat and flicked the taller ragman on the side of the face. The tall ragman held up his middle finger and screamed something about Cosmo's mother. Cosmo spit and pushed his hair out of his eyes. "I wonder if them bums have to practice to be that ugly?"

As the truck sputtered around the corner, Cosmo blew a pair of smoke streams from his nose and thought how great it would be to be rich. He meant rich! The kind of rich that when you opened your wallet a sweet-smelling leggy blonde would jump out of the pouch wrapped in hundreds. "I wish I was dirty rich," Cosmo said to nobody.

The truck swayed down Ninth Avenue, and Cosmo was becoming drowsy from the rocking motion. His eyes closed and suddenly flipped open every time the truck collided with a pot hole.

"Drive right or I'll smash ya!"

Cosmo was about to curse his brother's driving again when he saw the girl of his dreams. She was strictly top shelf . . . In this neighborhood her straw-colored hair was like a gold nugget set in the center of a bowl of dull iron bolts.

"Stop this crate!"

Victor down-shifted from third to second and Cosmo twisted out of the seat and balanced himself on the running board. As the truck angled toward the curb, he leaped to the sidewalk, reversed his direction and ran up to Annie O'Sherlock.

"Hey, Annie!"

"Thought you were in jail, Cosmo."

"Don't be cruel, Sugar . . . Can I offer you a lift with a gentleman?"

"Sure, d'you know where one is?"

"C'mon, dish, y'know I'm a very mannered fellow, you know that."

Annie slipped around Cosmo and continued down the street like she owned it. Cosmo watched her butt sway in the opposite motion of her shoulders and it made him want to bite his knuckles.

Matter of fact, he did bite his knuckles.

Cosmo had been trying to get in pretty with this tomato, but the only thing he had succeeded in doing was wasting a lot of wit.

Cosmo glanced across the street just as a fat lady heaved a pail of hot water on a sleeping bum two stories below.

Cosmo looked back up the street just as Annie approached the corner. To him, she was poetry in three-inch heels. It didn't matter to him that she wore enough make-up to plaster the entire Rockette chorus line. She had nice calves, she had Pizazz, she had everything except what she needed most. To Cosmo what she needed most was a little bit of himself wrapped around her body on a hot summer night.

Cosmo spat into his hand and tried to scrub some of the grime that had colored his skin the faint hue of old hospital walls. He ran toward her.

"Sweetness! Today was a great day—made a fortune—I'm shootin' up in this world."

"Yeah, you're a regular rocket, Cosmo."

Cosmo wanted to smile, but wasn't sure if his teeth looked classy enough this close to her eyes ... What blue lamps she had!

"So ya goin' places, huh?" Annie laughed warmly.

"Ya got the picture, dish," Cosmo said.

"Come on, Cosmo, I'm late."

"Hey, it's better I walk along."

"Why? You lonely?"

"The neighborhood here iz crawling with desperate characters."

"Answer me one thing."

"Spill, Doll."

"These characters that're crawling around the neighborhood—the desperate ones—they as desperate as you?"

"I ain't desperate, Sister, I'm in love!"

After Cosmo said this, he leaned forward for effect, hoping the sunlight would catch him at a certain angle and make his face nice.

"Ya breath's wiltin' my permanent."

Cosmo laughed as Annie put her hand on his chest and moved past the sweating con-man.

"Y'know, you're a snappy dish. Why're ya still hoofin' at that dump?"

"I don't hoof—I dance."

"Hoof— Dance, what's the difference. Ya still use ya feet— You don't deserve havin' them dime-a-dance creeps maulin' ya. A dish like yous should only be associatin' wid businessmen."

"Like you?"

"You got the drift, Sister."

"You got a lotta style for a guy with pigeon crap on his shoulder."

"That ain't real crap, I had it sewn on."

Cosmo refused to look at the pigeon waste that stuck to his uniform.

"When you gonna get a haircut?"

"It's my trademark, you know that," Cosmo said and

shook his head so his hair swung wide.

"Sugar, I feel it's my duty to finish this talk tonight. I'll be by Sticky's at the usual time."

"If you want."

" ... I'll be there."

Cosmo laughed. He liked her style. Even if she was breaking his horns, he liked her style.

Annie smiled at Cosmo, then bent over and straightened the seam of her stocking, then flipped her purse over her shoulder, and strutted away.

Knowing she was,

Next to the sun,

The hottest ball of gas in Hell's Kitchen.

Cosmo climbed back into the truck and slapped his brother's shoulder.

"Think my teeth need shinin'?—forget it—drive!"

3

EVERYONE IN HELL'S KITCHEN KNEW THE location of Giambelli's funeral parlor. It did not matter that the sign advertising his parlor had fallen down and broken two years before, because old Giambelli had earned the reputation of being able to box and bury you fast, cheap and quiet. The odds were that if, for some reason, you happened to drop dead in Hell's Kitchen, you'd be carted to Giambelli's and plopped on his doorstep. Sometimes Giambelli would find a stiff laying across his threshold with a note pinned to the corpse's coat requesting that it be buried quick and quiet before it started to stink, and usually there would be a twenty-dollar bill wound through the departed's fingers . . . Old Giambelli sat out front rocking in an old chair, drinking old wine, thinking old thoughts . . . Giambelli never talked, but in the young days it was different. In the young days Giambelli was a lively guy . . . He would smoke black cigars, talk loud and dance twice a week with his wife. Twenty-one years ago his wife died. She was the only body he ever refused to bury.

The ice truck finally arrived in front of Giambelli's funeral parlor and Victor killed the engine. Victor jumped down from the truck and landed on the balls of his feet, then turned back to look at Bella, who was in deep sleep and curled around the stick shift. Victor reached in and patted her back, then took hold of the two iron clamps that lay a foot away from the dog.

Victor started to whistle and walked past the side of the truck. He glanced down at the tire that was slowly becoming flat, then continued to the rear of the truck and opened the back doors. The sunlight that came in made Cosmo squint and he looked unhappy about the intrusion. Cosmo sat like a king on a throne of ice and was in no mood to have his cool peace disturbed by a pair of ice clamps and a grinning face.

"C'mom, I gotta go to work, Cosmo."

"Shut the doors, Jerk! Ya lettin' the good air out!"

"C'mon, jump down and lemme make a livin'."

Cosmo did not want to leave the cool belly of the truck and was quite content to be squatting on a canvas pad draped over a 200-pound block of ice. But he had to admit the freezing pain from the ice was beginning to burn his butt, so he decided to go along with his sweating brother's wishes.

"Go on, go to work ... I'm sick of rockin' around in this trashcan, anyway," Cosmo said.

Cosmo stood up, massaged his rear, and leaped from the truck. In a gray tee shirt, baggy army pants, wilting suspenders and a pair of exhausted white socks that hung over his heels, Cosmo Carboni stood in all his glory.

He glanced up at the sun, sneezed, and exploded with a well-primed wad of spit.

"Ain't Annie a dish?" Cosmo said.

"Yeah, she's pretty all right."

"She's got good strong legs an' built for a long race!"

Victor laughed and his deep voice echoed off the walls of the ice truck— Then bit the clamps into a pair of 150-pound blocks and dragged them from the tail of the truck.

"Need some help?"

"Sure!"

"Hire a partner," Cosmo offered and strode like a rooster across the pitted pavement in front of the funeral parlor, and stood in front of Giambelli. The old man sat there gray,

lined,

silent,

and rocking ... Giambelli was a restless statue.

"How much ice, Mr. Giambelli?" Victor asked respectfully.

" ... Wa?" Giambelli answered deafly.

"Ice! How much ice, pop!" Cosmo yelled.

" ... Justa two—justa two."

"Got that, Vic?—'Justa two,' " Cosmo said and entered the funeral parlor.

Even though the hallways were just barely wide enough for one man to move along, Cosmo got behind Victor, dipped below the ice, slipped past the iceman's knee and stood up in front of him.

"Whattaya doin', Cos?"

"I ain't walkin' behind nobody—I ain't nobody's fart catcher!"

Christ, Cosmo hated the smell of this place.

To him, the smell was a cross between damp plaster and dead hair. It was a gloomy hallway and only a very tired light bulb hung from a cord, but it was enough light to see the sick peeling brown walls and strings of dust webs that had sculptured themselves along the corridor's ceiling.

"Remind me to throw a party here someday," Cosmo said and belched.

At the end of the hallway, Cosmo again held open the door and Victor struggled through with the ice that was beginning to burn his shoulders.

"Say thank you."

"Thanks, Cos."

From across the room, the two brothers looked at their third brother, Lenny, working on a stiff. Lenny just glanced at his brothers and squinted slightly as the smoke from the cigarette hanging in the corner of his mouth stung his eye and continued up into his hair.

This room smelled even worse than the hallway.

Everything was made of wood and smelled like stale plaster. The plaster itself was dead and clinging with very little support from the ceiling. Sometimes a plaster chip would fall from above and land in a coffin only to be buried with the customer.

Cosmo figured that there was at least 300 pounds of the parlor's ceiling buried in graveyards around New York.

"What's buzzin', Lenny?"

Lenny shrugged at Cosmo and continued to work on the stiff.

"What's buzzin'?"

Lenny shrugged again and angled his words to Victor, who was standing against the room's other embalming table.

"Put the ice in the box, Victor."

Victor nodded and lumbered to the ice box in the rear of the room. Victor never minded taking orders from his handsome older bother. Lenny was the only person in Hell's Kitchen that treated him with something that felt like respect. But lately, Victor was feeling very unhappy because there had been a growing badness, an emptiness was in his older brother's eyes since he returned home from the war fourteen months ago. He thought maybe it was that Lenny's leg had been hurt bad and he had to walk with a cane. But he also figured there must be more to it than that because Lenny was tough. No, something else was bothering Leonard Carboni, but the iceman knew he was not smart enough to figure it out, so he didn't try—besides, it was too hot to think.

Cosmo walked over to where Big Lenny was working,

lifted up the sheet and stared at the body.

"Who's the stiff?"

"El Suppa."

Victor finished storing the ice and dug his hands into his pockets to get heat back into his fingers. He did not walk forward because no matter how many times he had been in this room, he did not like getting next to departed people.

"Who's El Suppa?" Victor asked from across the room.

Cosmo turned towards Victor then pulled the sheet off the dead man's face. "El Suppa! That corny organ grinder who worked the Irish neighborhood— Hey, Lenny, what happened to the old man's monkey?"

"Somebody took it."

"Whatta ya mean?"

"When El Suppa died, somebody swiped it."

"Iz that a fact?"

"That's a fact, Cosmo."

"Damn, I coulda used that ape."

"You never liked animals before, Cosmo," Victor offered.

"No, I ain't keen on that fleabag of yours, but El Suppa's monkey haz class!"

"There ain't no reason to call Bella a fleabag."

"Hey Vic, that mutt's got no class! If ya loved the animal, the nicest thing ya could do iz tie a rock around its neck an' throw it in the river."

"Don't be sayin' that, Cosmo!"

"Ahh, eat a worm! El Suppa's monkey haz real dancin'

talent that's worth big dough ... that creepy monkey coulda been a classy gimmick."

Cosmo was getting sick of debating with his brother, whom he considered nothing more than a large potato, and faced Lenny.

Before Cosmo could cock his lips and talk, an odor attacked his face and he held his nose and pointed at El Suppa. "Say, Lenny, ain't El Suppa gettin' a little ripe?"

" ... Ripe?"

"Better check his trousers for lumps, 'cause I think El Suppa waz so scared of dyin', he lumped in his pants!" After saying this, he held his nose and made a wrinkled face.

Lenny was getting annoyed and crushed out his cigarette.

"Why don't you take a walk," Lenny said.

"He stinks like fish!"

"Don't start, Cosmo!"

But all present knew it was too late, because once Cosmo had started it there was no stopping him unless he was to be knocked out, or you hired somebody to drop a piano on his head.

"Them grave diggers iz gonna think they's buryin' a crate fulla farts!" Cosmo said and made a "whew" sound.

Lenny did not like to hear this talk, but always expected it from Cosmo. A long time ago he had learned that Cosmo was a season that never changed.

Victor was unhappy and moved along the wall until he

was in a straight line with Cosmo. "Y'know, it ain't right bad-talking dead people."

"Whatta ya gruntin' about, Dunce?"

"Don't call me a dunce, okay?"

For the first time Lenny looked straight into Cosmo's eyes, "Why don't you leave him alone."

"That's okay, I ain't annoyed," said Victor.

"Where'd ya learn that word, *annoyed?*" asked Lenny.

Victor pushed away from the wall just enough to slip his hand into his back pocket and removed a flattened dictionary. "From this book ... Soon I'm going to get *academic.*"

Cosmo was sipping water from the sink faucet when he heard the word "academic," and the liquid sprayed from his mouth. "Academic!! And whoever said Vic ain't witty?" Cosmo yelled.

"You just won't give anybody a break."

"What're ya gettin' righteous for?"

"You, me, Victor, we're brothers ... doesn't that mean anythin' to you?"

"Yeah, there's a lotta bananas hangin' off our family tree."

"You got respect for nothin'," Lenny said in a dry voice.

"Hey, I got respect for the memory of Mama, John Garfield, an' me—that's it, brother."

After speaking, Cosmo smiled at Lenny.

It was a dim smile.

Cosmo knew his thin smile was drier than Lenny's

voice could ever be in a million years.

Cosmo walked over to Victor and draped his arm around the brother's shoulder. "C'mon, iceman, let's get some air—forget it, I wanna be alone."

Victor watched Cosmo leave, then he looked at Lenny.

He did not feel good about the way Cosmo had talked to Lenny.

He knew the ice in the truck was melting.

He knew his dog was getting lonely.

But he could not leave until he knew Lenny was not mad.

Victor walked over to the embalming table and unhooked Lenny's cane that hung from the table's side and handed it to his brother.

"Hey, Lenny, do Charlie Chaplin."

Lenny took his cane from Victor and spun it twice.

"Thanks, I'll see ya tonight."

Lenny watched Victor and Cosmo go and lit another cigarette. He took his cane from the edge of the table and limped across the room to straighten El Suppa's tie. After the tie was straightened, Lenny took out a bottle of whiskey that was in an empty coffin and removed a big history book from beneath the table and laid it on the dead man's stomach. He took a china cup from underneath the table and also placed it on the dead man's chest. He poured whiskey into the cup and, with the air of a gentleman, Lenny sipped and opened the history book to a marked page.

He studied the picture of a knight in, shining armor

slaying a dragon.

He was slightly self-conscious when he set down the cup, raised his cane like a sword and mimed the posture of the knight.

After a minute of daydreaming, he lowered his cane and replaced the history book.

He sipped away the remaining drops of whiskey and straightened El Suppa's tie again.

It was such a typical day.

4

THE SUN HAD BEEN TAKEN FROM THE SKY
and replaced by a hazy moon. The only memory of the
day that remained was the heat. It made the night air
heavy. Also at night there was not one square foot of
cement in Hell's Kitchen that did not have sound rising
from it. A radio hung from every window, a trash can lid
banged on every corner, a cat fight in every alley, a wino
gagged in every gutter. At night, Hell's Kitchen became a
symphony of racket without a conductor.

Annie O'Sherlock was dancing at the 'Sticky's
Ballroom.'
This was nothing new to her.
She had been hoofing there for the past two years, and
even though she didn't feel it was a great career move,
she somehow made herself believe that dancing would
keep her in touch with show business.
Annie O'Sherlock wanted show business.
Annie O'Sherlock wanted bright lights.

Annie O'Sherlock wanted every cliché that every pulp nickel rag sheet professed was the true American Dream.

All her life she had been giving. Giving to nameless men, giving to her mother who left her at thirteen to take off with some merchant marine, giving to her father who would work hard all week, go to church on Sunday, and try to molest his daughter on Monday.

When Annie was fourteen years old her old man had finally succeeded in downing enough rotgut to haul up the guts to corner his daughter in the kitchen. Annie had not known many facts about life. She did not know if it was wrong for her to scream, or scratch, or even to push her father's hands off her flesh. All she knew was that the closer her father came, the less he looked like her father.

He became a tan haze.

She could not focus on his features.

All Annie remembered from that evening was a cold floor, pain, the smell of wine, and pieces of her father's face caught under her nails. That night Annie became tough.

Yes, Annie was hoofing at Sticky's. The ballroom was nothing to write home about. It was tiny, dim, and jammed with smoke. All the girls were used to it. The only nice thing about Sticky's Ballroom was the red lights that shot down from the ceiling into the center, and when the red beams mixed with the smoke, it somehow gave the room the look of a foggy, magic place.

Annie was unquestionably the sharpest tomato there,

but her face was tired. The hustling instinct made her smile at the slob she danced with. But if you knew Annie, you knew from the eyes that her mind was very, very, very, very far away. But the mind would suddenly return to Sticky's Ballroom the instant a slob touched her curves or began to grind. Then Annie's eyes would become blue death threats, and the slobs would recognize in this sweet smelling thing lived something dangerous, something that a ten cent dance ticket was not worth getting involved with.

"Ya dime's up, ya time's up," Annie said and moved away from her faceless 'ten cent' partner and crossed the dance floor and joined a group of sore-footed dancers seated against the wall.

"How's things, Sweetie," an old hoofer asked.

"The same," Annie answered and sipped from her flask.

Fat Sticky oozed his weight over to the girls and pointed at the flask.

"Don't give the customers a hard time," Sticky said and smoothed his slick hair.

"He was pawin' me, Sticky," Annie said and sipped.

"So what? . . . An' no drinkin' on the dance floor—you know that."

"I'm healin' a broken heart, so get lost," Annie said wisely.

"Don't get fresh— C'mere."

Sticky drew Annie aside and pointed to a homely gent fingering his belt buckle on the other side of the room.

"The sucker'll give ya twenty bucks for a good time."

"Why don't you do it— Maybe ya'll get twenty cents— clean it up, Sticky," Annie said and flowed away.

Across the street was Mickey's Bar. As usual, the bar was stuffed with broad-backed working class guzzlers.
Nobody really enjoyed themselves in Micky's Bar.
They just floated from one brew to the next.
From one stool to the next.
From one dirty joke to the next.
Eventually they would stumble home with another hard day under their belts and hung over enough to tolerate the next day in Hell's Kitchen.
The barroom had dry-rotted away soon after World War I. The wood on the bar was warped and Mickey replaced it with sheets of aluminum that he painted flat brown. Five ceiling fans hung like stiff spiders over the drinkers, and when you got stinking drunk or bored enough, you could count the revolutions per minute. Some say it was fourteen. Some say it was fifteen. It depended on where you were sitting, or what you were drinking, or how rotten your brain was.
The Carboni brothers sat in a booth ... Ten empty beer bottles were lying across the tables and Cosmo was lecturing his other two brothers on the facts of life.
"The Carboni brothers! We wuz supposed to go places, but look at us ... A two-bit con-man, Victor hauls ice around like a friggin' Eskimo, an' you throw stiffs in a crate! ... A very classy crew."
Cosmo lapsed into quiet and the brothers sipped their booze and stared at the ceiling fans.

Victor stroked his dog that was under the table and wound around his right leg.

Lenny rolled his cane between his palms.

Cosmo belched.

Cosmo's cigarette was too short to hold and he crushed it against the side of the booth until it disappeared. He thought it would be swell to own a tobacco company.

"We're holdin' our own," Lenny defended.

"We're holdin' garbage!"

"Talk for yourself."

"I think we should rob somebody."

"I ain't robbin' nobody," Victor said and almost stood up. "You guys are causin' me to breathe heavy."

The debate ended when Cosmo saw something at the other end of the barroom that made him sit upright.

"Stop the music!"

"What?"

"It's Nickels Mahon's gang!"

" . . . So?"

"So they got El Suppa's monkey with them!"

Victor and Lenny turned to see Nickels Mahon and three of his gang coming through the door. The gang was dressed like rag bags and looked too young to be hanging around in Mickey's saloon. Nickels Mahon had quite a mug, featuring sunken cheeks, a weak spine and thin arms that were covered with sporty rags. His trademark was a cocked white hat and a matchstick in the corner of his mouth. Behind him stood the largest member of his gang and maybe one of the largest goons in New York. His name was Frankie the Thumper.

Frankie was a brute.

Frankie was dumb.

Frankie was a hurter.

On Frankie's monster shoulder perched El Suppa's missing monkey.

"I could make big dough with that monkey," Cosmo said in a drunken way.

"D'you see upon whose shoulder the monkey is perched?" Lenny asked.

"On Frankie the Thumper— So what?"

"So what?!"

"So what?!" Victor echoed.

"So what?" Cosmo said and was getting sick of hearing the phrase 'So what.'

"So get clever an' Mahon will have Frankie remove your face," Lenny said simply and sipped whiskey.

"Them bums swiped that monkey an' don't deserve to keep that creep."

"What d'you plan to do about it?" asked Lenny.

"Y'know how Nickels iz always sayin' nobody can beat Frankie the Thumper in arm wrestlin'?"

"We don't mix with the Mahons," Lenny said tightly.

"The trouble with you big brother iz ya weren't born with no sportin' blood."

Cosmo stood up and downed his beer in one swallow, tucked in his undershirt, flipped his hair back and swayed toward Nickels Mahon and his gang. "I got gallons of sportin' blood," Cosmo said to himself.

"Ya lookin' swell, Nickels ... Eatin' good lately?" Cosmo said, then felt very stupid for saying that. He snapped his fingers at Mickey and jerked towards Nickels. "Put a drink upon that gentleman!" Cosmo yelled too loudly.

Mahon tilted his head back and gave Cosmo the sleepy-eyed once-over, and it was easy to tell he was not fond of Cosmo's existence in Hell's Kitchen or on the planet earth.

"Getta haircut," Nickels snapped.

"Just got one. Look, if it was good enuff for Washington an' Tarzan to look like this, why not me, right?" Cosmo tried to joke.

"Whatta ya want?"

"Just shootin' the breeze."

"Shoot it somewhere else."

"How ya stay in such great shape, Nickels?"

"Avoidin' wops."

Cosmo knew he could snap Nickels in half with two fingers, but instead, used wit.

"I know what ya mean, the neighborhood's crawlin' with foreigners . . . Hey, Nickels, I remember once ya sez how Frankie could lick any guy in the neighborhood—I wanna know if ya still believe that tripe?"

Frankie the Thumper set down his beer. "Lookin' to get ya china punched out."

"Listen, I know ya a good scrapper, Frankie."

"Great wrestler!"

"Great . . . But my brother, Vic, who ain't so giant, iz strong as Charlie Atlas."

Nickels Mahon removed a cigarette that he had wedged behind his ear.

"Ya brother's a moron."

"That might be true."

"It's a fact!"

"He ain't no wit, but the first thing in the mornin' that young man can haul over 400 pounds of ice up five flights of stairs without blowin' his breakfast ... can you do that, Frankie?"

This time Frankie shoved Cosmo so hard that he bounced off the bar and staggered to the center of the room and collided with a short sailor.

Cosmo apologized to the sailor and looked at Frankie and thought the creep's neck had gotten bigger since the last time he had seen him. He also thought that Frankie was wearing padded shoulders, except that Frankie only had an undershirt on. Yeah, Frankie was a shaved ox in an undershirt.

"Hey, Frankie, don't start that puffin' an' punchin' stuff, huh."

"Beat it."

"C'mon, I'm just chewin' a friendly rag with Nickels here—right, Nickels?"

"I think ya suckin' wind."

"I ain't suckin' wind," Cosmo said, and thought about cutting Nickels' throat someday with the jagged edge of a bean can.

"Ya suckin' wind."

"Honest, I ain't suckin' no wind, Nickels."

"Then whatta ya got?"

" ... A gilt-edged business proposition."

*　　*　　*

Nickels Mahon and his gang traveled the room, shoving people aside until they were standing over Victor, who was tracing water rings on the table with his forefinger.

Cosmo eased his way through the gang and smacked Victor on the shoulder.

"Guess what?"

"What?" Victor said, but did not look up.

"Frankie here wants to have a friendly wrestlin' match with your arm."

Lenny leaned over to Victor and whispered in his ear, "You can still back out."

"Hey, who rattled your cage?" Cosmo said loudly.

"I'm lookin' out for Victor."

"Why don't ya go stand in the corner an' pretend ya popular!"

Mahon's gang shoved two drunks away from their table and pulled it to the center of the room. Nickels scratched his nose and yelled at Cosmo, "Let's go, wop!"

"Just a minute, Nickels," Cosmo said, and whispered into the iceman's ear, "Listen, I just bet a hundred bucks against that monkey. Of course, I ain't gotta dime ... Now if ya don't win, Vic, these creeps iz gonna drag ya into the alley and waltz in ya mouth."

"Let's go!" yelled Nickels.

Cosmo patted Victor's shoulder again and stood as Frankie the Thumper sat. Frankie handed the monkey to one of the smaller gang members, named Skinny the Hand.

Lenny limped to the bar, ordered a whiskey and

prepared to observe another stupid gimmick by his "witty" brother.

"I can't start yet," Victor said softly.

"Why not?!" Cosmo snapped. "Ya need an invite?!"

"I can't start until Bella is comfortable."

"Bella? Where iz that fleabag?"

Victor looked down and Cosmo reached under the table, grabbed Bella by the scruff and hauled the old dog to Victor. Victor pulled Bella into the booth next to him and stroked the dust from her side.

"Hey, what's ya mother doin' under the table?" Nickels yelled and laughed.

"Leave mothers out of it," Lenny said softly.

"What's that?" snapped Nickels.

"You heard me," Lenny said and limped to the bar.

"Ya ready, punk?" Frankie yelled in Victor's face.

"Y'know, the word 'punk' is a noun," Victor said with pride.

"Shut ya hole!"

"What say we get this friendly contest rollin'," Cosmo yelled and stepped back.

Victor felt nervous when the oily mountain sitting across from him curled back his lip and extended his hand to lock grips.

From the start, Frankie was out-muscling Victor and forced his arm a quarter of the way down.

Some of the guzzlers gathered around and were amused by the sight of these two horses trying to strain themselves to death. Cosmo tried to keep them from getting too close and breathing their stale breath on the combatants, but finally gave up and watched the contest from a bar stool.

Victor's hand was falling, and Nickels Mahon looked around for Cosmo until he found him.

He smiled and exposed his chipped tooth.

Nickels shook a fist at Cosmo and yelled loud enough for everyone to hear, "Ya better have that dough or you'll be spendin' a lotta time doin' a lotta healin'!"

The clock behind the bar read 10:30. Cosmo looked at the sweeping hand and wished he were invisible. He figured if he was invisible he could just float across the room real quietlike and cut Nickels' throat and nobody would never know who done it.

Cosmo slid off the stool and slid along the bar until he docked himself next to Lenny. "I wish I wuz invisible."

" ... Why?"

" 'Cause if I wuz—forget it."

5

ANNIE'S FEET BURNED AND HER EYES were sore from the low hanging clouds of stale smoke.

" ... I know the way other guys on the ship feel about women—"

Annie studied the clumsy dancer in the sailor's outfit, and wondered if she was jaded or going crazy. Because, as the young seadog spoke, she could see the words forming into distinct letters and falling out of the man's mouth and falling further still until the letters shattered silently on the floor. And they danced across this broken alphabet ... God, she was tired of everything, especially the lies.

"How's that?" Annie asked.

"You know— But I don't think the same way— I think women should have a guy show good manners ... if you have time, I'd like to show you my manners."

She knew it was coming. Why couldn't the wise guy be original, or better yet, honest.

"How many other girls have seen your manners?"

Annie said weakly and stopped cold when the band groaned the final note of 'Melancholy Baby.'

" ... Your dime's up—your time's up."

"How 'bout another dance?"

"Try another port."

Annie walked away and joined the line of tired hoofers leaning against the wall.

"Everybody's got an angle," she said and sipped.

"Ya got what they want, honey."

"I'm not givin' nothin' away."

"Sell it—take the money."

A customer with a shiny suit waddled over and handed Annie a ten cent ticket.

"What's your angle?"

"What?"

"C'mon, just dance."

6

COSMO KNEW HE AND HIS BROTHERS stood an odds-on chance of being waltzed into the alley and given a professional face ache that would last them the rest of the summer. He remembered the time he saw Nickels Mahon's gang maul an Italian bum New Year's Eve, 1944.

Nickels clobbered the bum from behind with a trash can lid and that took the starch out of the bum's legs. He saw the shortest gang member, a jerk named Pigpen, chop a sawed-off broomstick across the bum's neck that laid him flat. Skinny the Hand and Pigpen stretched the bum out, and Frankie thumped his ribs in. Even from his hiding place across the street, Cosmo heard the way it sounded—the way raw spaghetti sounds when snapped in half. He heard the derelict mumbling something about Jesus and St. Christopher and how he was sorry. Cosmo could not figure out what the slob was sorry for. Living?

Again, the bum screamed he was Catholic and a tax-
payer and a veteran and the father of twenty kids and
any other lie to save his life. Nickels Mahon said he
didn't give a damn and twisted his heel into the man's
mouth. The bum's gray teeth broke out and made that
special sound that only teeth make when they are being
kicked out and fall onto wet cobblestone. But the sound
Cosmo remembered best was when Skinny the Hand and
Pigpen grabbed the bum's legs and pulled in opposite
directions until the hip sockets popped like a bottle of
warm soda. Cosmo was sick to his stomach, but watched
anyway. He wanted to jump up and call them sons of
Canal Street whores and bite their faces, but he was
smart enough to be quiet.

Cosmo sat and watched.

He watched until Frankie dragged the bum over to the
curb and rammed the unshaven face down on a fire plug,
until half the blunt point disappeared into the bum's
head.

Cosmo looked at the bum.

In the gutter, he thought the bum looked like a pile of
rags ... a dead pile of red rags.

The crowd of guzzlers had become larger and they all
looked amazed because Victor's arm was angled three
inches above the tabletop and had not budged in more
than an hour.

Lenny studied the fear in Cosmo's face then limped
over to Victor. He leaned next to Victor's ear and spoke

with softness in his voice. " ... Victor, you can win. You can win because I believe in you, Cosmo believes in you, and Mom and Dad, wherever they are, believe in you. Now, d'you believe in yourself? ... Win ... Win ... Win."

Victor applied all his strength and his arm slowly began to rise, and the crowd started making noise and laying more bets.

Lenny continued to chant, "Win, win, win, win," and the iceman's arm arched higher and higher and Frankie's face twisted in pain, his eyes were falling out of his face.

Cosmo yelled that his brother was Charles Atlas and started laughing hysterically.

Everyone standing close to Cosmo figured the young Italian had warped his brain by screaming too loud.

Frankie's arm buckled and smashed against the top of the table, loud enough to rise above all the other noise in the room.

Frankie slumped against the booth.

And made the face of a loser.

Cosmo screamed even louder and snatched a mug of beer off the bar and slammed it in front of Victor.

"Great show, Vic!"

Cosmo spied Nickels heading towards the men's room and cut him off.

"Nice try, Nickels. Where's the monkey?"

"Get it from Pigpen."

Nickels thumbed over his shoulder and Cosmo turned and saw Pigpen holding the monkey under his arm like it

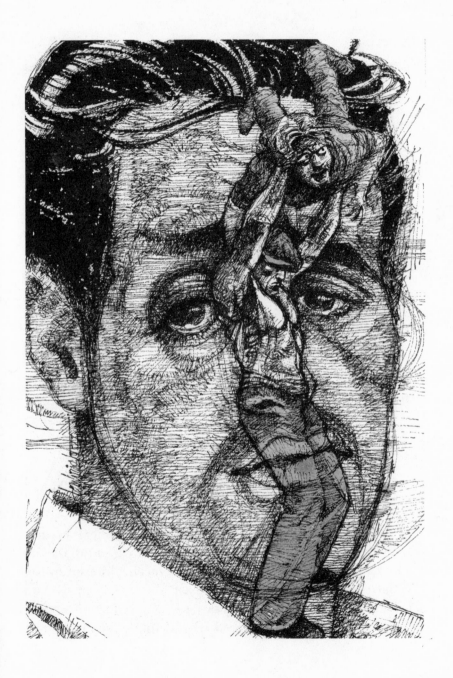

was a hairy lunch pail. Christ, Pigpen had a hard face.

A stinking face.

An ugly face.

A rotten face.

The kind of face you wanted to drive a steam roller over, and over, and over, etc.

"Hey, Pigpen, hand over the animal."

Cosmo tried to snag the monkey, but Pigpen whipped out a knife and stuck it up to Cosmo's neck, "The monkey belongs to me," Pigpen said with a lisp that sprayed foul-smelling juice on Cosmo.

"It might look like ya, but it don't belong to ya, Pig. Put the blade away before ya have it for dinner."

Pigpen hated the way Cosmo was acting brave with a knife to his neck, and pushed the blade harder.

A right hand clenched Pigpen's throat. The other hand gripped the crotch, and Victor lifted him over his head. Pigpen screamed and begged, but all the guzzlers yelled for his blood ... Everybody wanted Victor to smash the punk against the wall.

Victor tensed and felt his veins coming out.

Victor did not like to hurt people, but this was not the same.

It had to be done. It was a kind of biblical justice. Victor arched his back and was about to catapult the punk against a wooden beam, when he saw himself in the mirror. He had never seen himself like this. Nobody had seen him like this. He also saw Lenny's reflection appear in the mirror and wondered why Lenny's face looked so afraid.

"Put him down, Victor."

Victor obeyed Lenny's command and lowered Pigpen to the floor.

Pigpen was crying and the front of his pants were wet.

Nickels Mahon and his gang wanted to start trouble, but did not like the way the crowd was staring at them and decided to take a hike and not heckle the Carboni Brothers.

Cosmo came over stroking his monkey and slapped Victor on the shoulder, "That wuz great, Vic, 'cept ya shoulda made a wish with his legs. C'mon, let's celebrate!"

Before Victor could say anything, Cosmo swayed over to the bar followed by a herd of guzzlers.

Victor was still very confused by all the excitement and touched Lenny's arm. ˙

"Lenny, I didn't want to hurt him. Pigpen wanted to be hurt."

"Guys like Pigpen always wanna be hurt."

" . . . I'm gonna get some ice cream," Victor said.

Lenny smiled and Victor took hold of Bella's collar and helped her off the floor. As they walked towards the exit, they had to move along the bar and nearly everyone in Mickey's patted Victor's shoulder and offered congratulations. At first, it kind of scared him, because no one had ever said so many nice things to him at one time, but he started to like it, and by the time he left the bar, he was grinning.

Cosmo leaned against the bar and kissed his monkey. Tonight was his night and he felt like broadcasting his thoughts in a loud voice. "Y'know, sometimes I wonder about nature. I'm tough an' nervy, but my kid brother, who should be a real rough pecker, iz about as mean as a daisy ... Don't ya guys ever wonder 'bout nature? Yeah, nature's a funny thing—Anybody gotta smoke?"

Mickey the bartender grinned and tossed Cosmo a smoke. He usually wouldn't give the young man a cigarette, but tonight it was different.

Cosmo lit the cigarette and leaned over to Mickey and spoke just loud enough for him to hear.

"Hey, Mick ... Ya wanna buy a monkey?"

7

HELLO, VIC . . . THE USUAL?"

Victor nodded at the soda jerk and flipped through an old copy of *Look* magazine, laying on the worn marble counter. The soda jerk scratched his red nose and snatched a look at Bella, who was sleeping at Victor's feet.

"Hey, Vic, everyday, rain or shine, ya come in here an' buy a vanilla cone, then give it to ya dog . . . How come?"

" 'Cause she don't like chocolate."

The soda jerk handed Victor the cone and wondered if the iceman's answer was on the level or if he was just trying to be a smart aleck. He guessed that the iceman was just in one of his dumb moods and took the nickel from Victor and flipped it into the cash register . . . It bounced out.

Victor nudged the old dog and she followed him outside.

Just as Victor was about to sit on the stoop outside

the soda shop, Nickels Mahon and his gang came around the corner.

"Hey, screwball, we got business together," Nickels said, and stood in front of Victor.

Victor did not bother to look into Nickels' eyes and just sat next to Bella and watched the dog lap the ice cream cone. The gang gathered around and formed a wall of meat in front of Victor.

"Ya cheated Frankie."

"I didn't cheat nobody," Victor said and Nickels twisted his heel on Victor's foot. Victor ignored the pain and continued to watch Bella lap the vanilla mess.

"We been discussin' ramming ya face on a fire plug, whatta ya think about that?"

There was something in the way Nickels said those words that made Victor smile. Skinny the Hand stuck his crooked forefinger close to Victor's face and hissed, "Maybe ya like ya shins busted wid a broom handle?! Whatta ya think about that?"

Victor smiled again and Nickels got so mad he changed color and spit. "Whatta ya grinnin' at?" Nickels yelled.

"Frankie's makin' faces at me," Victor said softly.

"Lemme dent his face!" Frankie bellowed and shook his fist under Victor's nose.

"Ya fists iz too valuable to waste on this dope," Nickels said.

Victor saw the last of the ice cream cone disappear into his dog's mouth and he lifted her into his arms and started to walk away.

"Goodnight," he said over his shoulder.

Nickels was going to heave an empty can that he saw laying in the gutter at the departing iceman, but as he bent over, he saw Annie O'Sherlock and two other tarts between his legs.

Nickels didn't have to say a word.

He just stood up, swayed across the street and the pack of stacked rats fell in behind the girls. Employing his crippled wit to the fullest, Nickels reached into his pocket, retrieved several coins, and started tossing dimes at the girls' feet.

"There's my dime ... Now how 'bout a dance, Hot Stuff?"

The girl on the right side of Annie had giant teeth and she exposed this mouth full of china, and wrinkled her painted lips. "You're a real class act, Nickels!" Giant Teeth said.

"Clam up, I'm talkin' to Annie O'Sherlock ... What say you an' me goin' in the alley?"

Annie had always enjoyed the way men's eyes wandered over her form, and Nickels Mahon had been trying to crawl beneath her linen for at least six years, but so far it was a strain for her to even give the Irish dirtball the time of day. Anybody in the neighborhood knew that when you got connected with Nickels Mahon, it was strictly cheap thrills.

"Hey, what say you an' me go in the alley?"

"We came out to get some fresh air, Nickels."

"C'mon, Doll, whatta ya savin' ya brownie for, the worms?"

"Hey, Nickels, I'm tired and don't want any trouble."

" . . . I don't work an' I am trouble."

"You're a jerk."

"Bad-talk me an' I'll—"

"What? Smack me around?—Go ahead, I'm gettin' bored."

Mahon let her go and Annie and the girls sneered at Nickels and climbed the steps to Sticky's.

"Ya's better go before I slap ya's all around— Let's go."

"Where?" Frankie asked.

"Let's climb a hooker at the Sunset Hotel."

8

ROSE SAT ON HER STOOP PASSING TIME. She was a full-blooded Italian and had an unusual face that was almost hidden behind a bland hairdo. She fanned herself from the street heat, and every few seconds looked up and down the block.

Rose was a pleasant person. Few things on earth ever got under her skin. To her life was simple. She did not want wealth, or sex with blond men, or long legs, she only wanted to be married and share someone else's life.

Rose looked down at her feet and wrinkles grew across her forehead. Everytime she glanced down at the straw shoes she bought three weeks ago and saw her big toe easing through a worn spot at the tip, she got mad. These were the only new shoes she had bought in two years and she felt angry every time she looked down and saw the toe.

"Hello, Bella ... Well, what's with the long face tonight, Victor?" Rose asked and motioned for him to sit.

" ... dunno why my face is long," Victor said.

"C'mon, what's the matter with lil' Vickie tonight?"

"Confusion."

"What confusion?"

Victor shrugged and looked up the block just in time to see a bum stagger into a pool of light beneath a street lamp. The drunk bum did a little dance, jumped into the air, and crashed into the gutter.

"Sometimes I don't like this place much," Victor said.

"It don't matter. We're getting out soon."

"Y'know, I keep thinkin' how good it's gonna be when we get that houseboat in New Jersey."

"When do you think we'll have enough money?"

"A few years ... Eight years."

"Then I have time to pack," Rose said and smiled.

Victor looked down and started to laugh hard.

"What's so funny? Tell me!"

"I can't!" Victor said and laughed harder.

"What's so funny?"

"Your toe looks like a thumb!"

Rose looked down at the sight she had seen a hundred times that day. Her big toe easing through the worn spot in her straw shoe did resemble a flat, crooked thumb.

"Enough, Vickie!"

"Sorry, Rose," Victor said and bit his lip to stop laughing.

"Forget it ... Now, tell me something nice."

"Whatta ya want to hear?"

"Tell me what you tell me every night."

" ... Say it now?" Victor said shyly.

"Right now."

"But I just finished laughin'."

"Say it now or you'll hurt my feelings."

" ... I love you, Rose."

Victor leaned forward and Rose stroked the whiteness of his neck, but the iceman could not take his eyes from the worn spot in her shoe.

"Y'know, ya toe really does look like a thumb," Victor said softly.

" ... And your head looks like a meat-loaf," Rose replied almost romantically.

They started to laugh together, but before their laughter could reach a peak, Rose's mother leaned from the window three stories up.

"Rosa, yew come-a to bed ... Hellooo, Vittorio!"

"Hello, Mrs. Menetti."

"Gotta go."

"Yeah, I figured that."

"See ya tomorrow."

Rose kissed the iceman and stroked the old dog, and disappeared into the tenement doorway.

Victor looked down the street to see if the dancing bum was still stretched in the gutter.

He was.

Victor shook his head and thought about how much he did not like this place anymore. He hoisted his dog and walked home.

9

COSMO GROUND OUT HIS CIGARETTE WITH a sharp twist of his heel and gathered the rope of dance tickets into his hand. Then, cocking his hat, swayed towards Annie.

"Every night like clockwork, huh— I know ya dogs are tired, so ya just hang on to my neck— Nice neck, huh— Washed it last week ... ya suppose to smile— Forget it. Ya just hang on to Cosmo here an' I'll drag ya around for the rest of the night."

Annie smiled in a tired way and put both her arms around Cosmo's neck and let him drag her away.

Lenny finished his brew and stepped out of Mickey's Bar ... He took two deep breaths and started down the block. But he stopped and rubbed the handle of his cane and looked up at Sticky's Ballroom. He felt the music floating down to the street and he watched bodies, coated in red lights, floating past the window ...

Lenny tapped his cane and started home again.

10

THE MOON WAS ON ITS WAY DOWN WHEN
Annie and Cosmo turned the corner of her block.

"The way I see it is this—we hire a ten—no, twenty
piece band an' I'll set ya up at the best club in Manhat-
tan, or Brooklyn, if ya want—no, forget Brooklyn, I don't
want ya dancin' in no ship-yard—"

" . . . Stop Cos', I'm too tired to laugh."

"Why don't ya lay down here an' I'll wake ya up in
the mornin' an' we'll finish this deal."

"No, go on."

Cosmo cleared his throat and almost spit. Instead he
swallowed and pulled a smoke out of his hat.

"When are you gonna wash your hair?" Annie asked
teasingly.

"What's the matter?" Cosmo defended, "Looks like I
comb my hair with a pork chop— Hey, long oily hair
proves ya brain is workin' — Show me a guy with short
dry hair, an' I'll show you an idiot."

"The mouth never stops."

"It's my fortune—listen, we getta band, work up an act, get ya dressed up in alotta feathers and red beads. Then we set out. I'll handle the paper work; an' we smash every record in the country. 'Annie O'Sherlock and Her Red Hot Dancing Legs!' —I'm tellin' ya, we couldn't miss."

"Can't huh?"

"Can't—impossible."

Annie stopped in front of her steps and looked idly at the aging building that looked like it was trying to find a quiet way to crumble . . . Cosmo glanced down the empty street.

"Kinda nice with all the riff-raff pigs off the street."

Annie nodded and leaned forward to place a kiss on his cheek.

"Ya eyes need glasses."

"Why?"

"You keep missin' my mouth." Cosmo said and grinned as Annie touched his face and climbed the steps.

11

THE FOLLOWING MORNING COSMO ROSE TO greet the rain that splattered into the basement apartment through a small angular window.

He sat on the edge of his bed resembling a large laundry bag because he was still garbed in the clothing he was wearing the night before.

The basement was jammed with an ocean of junk that Cosmo had collected from around the neighborhood. Often the brothers griped to Cosmo that the room was becoming a filth trap, but he defended the garbage by saying the merchandise stored in his room would, in about a hundred years, be worth a fortune.

The room was painted gray because four years ago Cosmo swiped two gallons of gray paint from a truck parked behind Lunatics' Hospital.

Cosmo swiveled his sore eyes and looked at Lenny sleeping on a stack of flat mattresses. Lenny's history book, cane and bottle lay at his side. Cosmo wondered how his older brother could sleep like a normal person, but never get his hair messed up.

Cosmo then shifted his eyes over to Victor. Victor slept on a stack of seven straw mattresses that Cosmo had also found outside the hospital. He watched Victor stir and finally stretch his muscles until his body became a straight, yawning line. Victor kissed the dog laying beside him and musically whispered into the dog's sagging face.

"Bella, Bella, Bella, wake up and eat, eat, eat," Victor sang flatly.

"Christ! D'ya have to start off every mornin' by croonin' to that mutt?" Cosmo rasped.

"Bella likes to hear music in the mornin'," Victor said without much force.

"Then buy the fleabag a radio!"

Cosmo lowered his other foot to the floor and fumbled beneath the bed for his shoes until he realized they were already on his feet. He groaned as he rose and swayed to the window sill and watched the monkey lapping rain water off the window sill and wondered what the hell he was going to do with this ape. If he owned an oven, he would most likely cook it. Cosmo stroked the monkey's brittle fur and dabbed rain water on his sleep-crusted eyes. Yawning, he stared out at the drizzle and the sticky brick-redness of Hell's Kitchen.

"Looks like rain," Cosmo said softly to himself.

12

COSMO STOOD IN THE MOUTH OF AN ALleyway trying to unload a load of umbrellas, but people just passed by and smiled. The sky had cleared and Hell's Kitchen was once again covered in yellow hotness.

Cosmo had opened the umbrellas and displayed them in a semi-circle and moved in and out of the umbrellas like he was rehearsing a bad nightclub act.

"Umbrellas here! They're goin' very fast!"

An old Italian with a shoeshine kit shuffled past and Cosmo grabbed the man by the crook of his arm. "Here's a man who could use a new umbrella."

"No needa umbrella—" the old man said, and eyed Cosmo's hair. "You a boy or a girl?"

"Whatta ya say, Pop? For a buck ya can't go wrong."

"No needa umbrella."

"Boy—seventy-five cents! It'll keep ya brain dry."

"No needa umbrella."

"How 'bout fifty cents?"

" ... No."

"All right. Two-bits an' a free shine."

" . . . One shoe."

"Shine one shoe?! Whatta 'bout the other shoe?"

" . . . Twenty-five cents more."

"That means I end up givin' you a free umbrella! Beat it, ya cheap creep, before I tear up your passport!"

The old man shrugged and shouldered his shoe shine kit and rambled away from Cosmo just as Nickels Mahon and his gang came tilting around the corner, towing a small Italian gent with a heavy mustache.

Cosmo cursed himself for not staying in bed this morning.

"Hey, my friend, Nickels Mahon!" Cosmo said, "Hey Nickels, how 'bout a nice umbrella?"

"How much?"

"For you . . . Two dollars."

Nickels Mahon shifted the matchstick from one corner of his mouth to the other, winked at his gang, then pulled the small Italian man from behind Frankie the Thumper. "I wanna introduce ya to Pop Vito," Nickels said with an air of forced street formality.

"Sure, I know Mr. Hair."

" . . . Pop Vito has a problem this mornin'," said Nickels.

"Who don't?" Cosmo replied.

Pop Vito was unable to contain his tiny temper any longer and grabbed Cosmo by the ragged sleeve of his undershirt and spit out the words in broken Italian.

"Nine-a o'clock-a this mornin', ten goddamn'a customer-a in my barber shop—dey getta hair cutta, all-a sudden."

Before Pop Vito could continue to plague everyone's ears with his squeaky broken English, Nickels Mahon wrapped a hand over his mouth, "Clam up, ya emigrant! Okay, wop, what it iz iz dis—dis greaseball has accused me of thievin' his umbrellas."

"Yeah?"

"Yeah. But we both know who really done it, don't we?"

Nickels Mahon and his gang saved Cosmo from bothering to come up with an alibi by jumping on and mutilating all of the umbrellas with great professional care. Pop Vito babbled crazy Italian until Skinny the Hand grabbed him by his mustache and flung the barber against a stack of crates. The little dago suddenly got a rush of guts to the head and pushed a hole through the gang, snatched up the broken remains of his customers' umbrellas and stormed away, yelling something about communists.

"Thanks, Nickels, I wuz thinkin' of retirin' anyway," Cosmo said and started to inch away.

"Hey, dis don't mean we's even, either."

"How's that?"

"Ya still gonna get it for hurtin' Frankie's feelin's last night . . . Right, Frankie?"

Frankie moved fast for a big man and Cosmo was wondering how he could have been knocked on his butt without having ever seen the meaty hand that pushed him. Cosmo looked up at the circle of eyes that stared down at him and knew at the slightest show of nerve, these creeps would be more than happy to grind his body into the pavement until he was nothing more than a wet spot on the sidewalks of New York.

Cosmo had wit.

"Nice," Cosmo said and rose to one knee.

"What wuz?" Frankie the Thumper said in a dry voice.

"The shove! Y'know, every mornin' I can't wait to wake up an' run outside just so I can be bruised by you, Frankie . . . Thanks, someday maybe I can make yours."

"What's that mean?"

Cosmo shrugged and looked up at the sky. The sun was blasting through a maze of hanging laundry and its power made Cosmo squint and shade his eyes with the side of his hand.

" . . . Great day for the beach," Cosmo said, and strolled nimbly away.

13

LENNY HAD SIPPED HIS 86-PROOF BREAK-
fast at Mickey's joint and now limped to work ... He
passed many familiar faces that wanted to say hello, but
Lenny kept his eyes on the cement until he arrived at
the Giambelli Funeral Parlor ...

When Lenny put his key in the door, he saw something slumped behind a trashcan. Lenny licked his lips
and limped over to the corpse and touched the man with
his cane ... Lenny bent forward and read the note with
the twenty-dollar bill attached. It read: "Bury him fast."

The landlord screamed at a pair of mick brats that
almost tripped him as he strained to haul his bulk up the
stairs to Annie's apartment.

Annie poured another glass of wine and continued to
chisel on a wood statue that was starting to resemble
Cosmo. The many other wood carvings around the room
were good, damn good, but she never wanted to sell

them. She would rather have them stack up than give them out to the broads at Sticky's.

The radio's music almost drowned out the landlord's knock, but not quite. Annie dropped the chisel, picked up her smoldering cigarette and opened the door.

"The rent, right?" she asked, knowing the answer.

"It's time—thirty dollars," the landlord said between heavy breaths.

"Did the rats pay?"

"What rats?"

"The rats livin' in this apartment," Annie said and took a couple bills out of her pocket. "This was supposed to be a private room—but since I'm sharin' it, I'll pay half an' get the other half from the rats."

"Wait—maybe we can work somethin' out," the landlord said and scratched his ribs.

"How's that?"

"Maybe tonight I could—"

"Everybody's got an angle—everybody's a lover—Look, let's keep it a mystery."

Annie walked to the radiator and picked up the small wood statue of a fighting cat, and handed it to the landlord.

"Here's fifteen dollars an' a statue—enjoy," Annie said, and slammed the door.

14

VICTOR BRAKED THE ICE TRUCK IN FRONT
of Giambelli's funeral parlor, stepped out and lowered his
old dog to the sidewalk. He flipped two burlap pads over
his shoulders then hoisted a pair of blocks and swung
them atop the pads and approached Mr. Giambelli, who
was rocking as usual.

"Mornin', Mr. Giambelli."

"Justa two ice in da back— Justa two."

Cosmo was standing in the embalming room running
his hands along the silk lining of a walnut coffin when
Victor and his dog came through the door.

Cosmo was not startled and still rubbed the smooth
coffin liner, as his monkey sat on the window sill search-
ing his body for fleas.

"Greetin's," Cosmo said with a grin.

"Where's Lenny?" Victor asked, lowering the ice.

"Wrappin' his teeth around some lunch."

Victor watched Cosmo fire up a cigarette and nearly devour the thing in three noisy drags. Victor noticed that Cosmo was draped in a baggy black suit, the kind of suit he was sure Lenny used to dress cadavers for cheap funerals.

"Hey, where'd ya get the new duds?"

"Won 'em in a raffle," Cosmo casually replied.

Victor let his eyes wander to a pine board coffin balanced between a pair of saw-horses. He walked over to the coffin and looked down. The corpse was in his underwear. The man was not old, but had been growing bald, and Victor could tell from the black fingers that he was either a mechanic or a bootblack, or maybe just a dead guy with filthy hands.

"Why're ya lookin' like a piece of chewed string?" Cosmo asked and ground out his cigarette.

"Raffle nothin', ya swiped that man's suit!"

"C'mon, Vic, why should I walk around lookin' like a boiled rag when I can have a snappy set of duds for free?"

"Ya swipin' from the deceased!"

"Listen, this guy come into the world nude as a needle, so I think it's only fittin' that that's the way he go out."

" . . . It ain't polite."

"C'mon, I figger when ya gone, ya gone, right?"

"That's true."

"True, right, so why be fancy an' wear a suit? I mean, iz this stiff goin' dancin' or somethin'?"

"No— He ain't goin' dancin'."

"But I am, an' can't afford to look like no Eastside punk tonight, okay, Vic?"

"Ya gotta return it when ya done."

"Sure, first thing in the mornin' ... Now, I wanna show ya somethin' important— Bring ya face into that room."

Cosmo was the first to enter the small room at the end of the parlor that Lenny sometimes used to store embalming fluid, but Lenny also used the room to keep cadavers when traffic was heavy.

Cosmo flicked on the light, fired up another cigarette, then flipped back the sheet covering a cadaver.

Before the sheet fell to the floor, Victor saw the face of a red-haired woman.

"Now, I wuz cookin' up a gimmick to scrape up a few bucks, an' since ya my brother, I'm gonna let ya in on this genius gimmick."

"Who is she?"

"Don't ya recognize that kisser?"

" ... No."

"This iz Sloppy Suzy from the Sunset."

"I don't know her," Victor said and felt a little nervous.

"C'mon, this iz Sloppy Suzy— She was one of the hookers hawkin' their brownies over at the Sunset Hotel."

"What happened to her?"

"Last night, this tomato dipped into some bad Chinatown junk an' dropped dead for the last time."

" ... Cover her, Cosmo."

"The Suz iz peachy stiff, would you agree?"

"Cover her, Cosmo."

"Hey, she ain't gonna catch a cold— Listen, tonight I'm gonna unlock this joint an' slip in here with Suzy ... Now for the business end."

"I don't wanna hear no business end."

"Clam up an' listen ... I'm gonna go out an' round up some winos, see— A herd of winos— Then we charge the slobs two bits a piece for a ride on Suzy."

"But she's dead!"

"We tell 'em she's a heavy sleeper— They'll believe it 'cause them bums'll be drunk enough to dip their wick in anythin'!" Cosmo said in one breath.

"But she's departed!"

"Hey, I know she's departed!—I got eyes!— She ain't here for a vacation!— This ain't no social call— She's dead—stiff—defunct— Why else would she be here! Now the slobs come in and we take their two bits and throw them in the saddle. Whatta ya say, Vic?"

" ... Ya crazy."

"That's what they sez about Edison ... Now, tonight's our only night, 'cause Suzy's goin' in the box by noon."

"Cos—"

"Don't talk, just listen. Tonight's our only night to cash in on Suzy's profession, an' ya know, I really feel in my heart that she wouldn't mind ... "

Victor kept looking at Suzy and thought that she looked angry the way her red hair swung around the

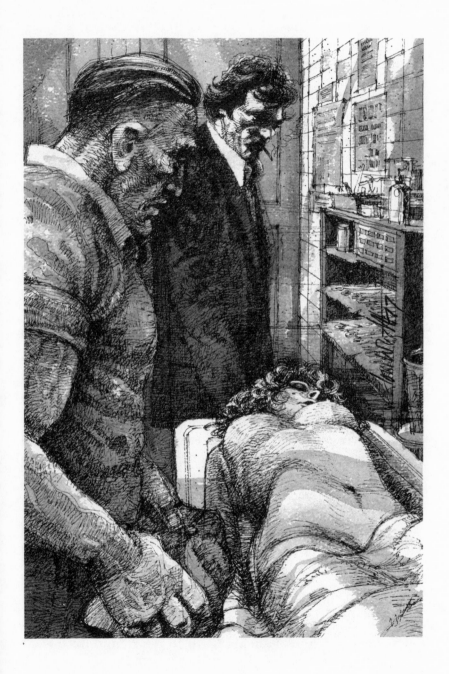

white face like a gust of bloody wind and her lips looked like they were trying to say something.

Victor wanted to pick her up and wrap her in a sheet and

Run out of the room,

Run down the hall,

Jump over the cracked pavement

And leap into his truck. He thought it would be a righteous act to save Suzy from Cosmo's gimmick and did not care if she had "hawked her brownie" at the Sunset Hotel.

Victor had already figured out how he could help Suzy. He would cover her with blocks of ice in the truck and she could stay fresh. That night when he drove back to the warehouse, he would sneak her into the main ice house. He knew a special corner in the ice house. It was way in the back and no one ever went there at all because they were afraid of getting locked in. Because three years ago the assistant foreman had gone in there to check for heat drafts and somebody accidentally shut the door, and when they found him frozen the following morning, he was sitting cross-legged in the corner with his clipboard in his lap ... No one ever found his pencil, though.

"Well, lil' brother, whatta ya say?"

" ... Don't do it."

"Ya killin' my enthusiasm."

"Don't do it, Cosmo— Go steal somethin' instead."

" ... Yeah, mebbe ya right— Listen, I gotta date tonight— Y'know I should learn to relax from business."

Victor wanted to look at Cosmo, but could not. All he could do was glance down at Bella and Bella followed him to the door, down the hallway and out to the street.

Cosmo watched his brother go and lit another cigarette and looked down at Suzy and shrugged.

" ... Just kiddin', Suz."

15

THAT EARLY EVENING, COSMO AND HIS monkey stood on the corner of 47th and Eighth Avenue trying to drum up some business. The monkey wore a faded carnival hat, and Cosmo was enthusiastically grinding a hand organ, and dressed in the baggy funeral suit. Why the monkey just wanted to squat on the sidewalk and pick fleas from his mangy body, nobody knew.

Cosmo yanked the chain, but the animal wanted to scratch. The young con-man was beginning to suffer embarrassment as punks passed by and laughed.

"Dance, don't scratch! Dance!"

Unfortunately for Cosmo the monkey did not speak English and now picked its toes.

"Dance!—I'll kill ya! I'll kill ya!"

Cosmo was just working into a sweat when a dime landed at his feet.

"Hey, Annie, I'm glad ya passed by!" Cosmo said and tried not to redden.

"Why?" Annie said and eyed the funeral suit.

" ... Ahhh, I just got this job teachin' monkeys to dance— Part time."

"Special work, huh?— Plan on makin' a fool of yourself all night?"

"Just for a few hours—matter of fact I'm sick of this bum gimmick—ever eat a monkey? Where ya goin'?"

"Work."

"I'll see ya at Sticky's."

"Listen—you don't always have to come by—if ya have something else to do."

"No, I wanna— I'll see ya later."

Annie nodded and waited for the traffic to clear, then moved quickly across the street. Cosmo watched her disappear into the flowing humanity of the neighborhood, then bent down and grabbed the monkey by the back of the neck ... "You got nothin' goin', creep."

16

VICTOR WAS HARD AT WORK IN THE MAIN freezer at the ice house depot. He wore a heavy, fraying coat and wool cap that was pulled over his ears. Steam jetted from his mouth as he stacked hundred-pound blocks of ice in neat columns that rose to the ceiling.

Victor heard the door open and saw the foreman's square face lean inside. The foreman was a heavy Pole with a thick stomach and thick accent to match. He had been around ice so long that he now looked like a three-hundred-pound block. With his face still hanging in the doorway, his hand lifted a sandwich to his mouth, the teeth ripped off a hunk, and mayonnaise stuck to his upper lip.

"Time to go home— You werk hard tewday, Victor."

"I work hard 'cause I want to escalate, Mr. Vitvitsky."

"Vat's dis escalate?"

Victor shoved the final block into place and looked at the foreman.

"I could use a small raise, Mr. Vitvitsky."

The foreman's teeth ripped off another piece of the sandwich, then he moved a small wad of money from his shirt pocket, counted out a few bills, and smacked them on a block of ice. He took a coin from his pocket and placed it on top of the bills.

"Here's yew pay, Victor . . . Since you werk harder den anybody, I give yew a raise . . . Here fifteen dollar for veek, and twenty-five zent raise."

The foreman slammed the door and Victor idly traced figure eights on a smooth block. He stared down at the meager sum laying on the ice.

"Twenty-five cents ain't an escalate."

17

THE MOON THAT HUNG OVER THE HUDSON River gave off just enough light to outline Victor and Rose sitting on the end of an old wharf.

Rose appeared calm and content just to watch Victor tearing rotten pieces of wood off the wharf and tossing them at a floating can.

" . . . Vickie, are you happy?"

"Sure, I'm happy."

"How come I don't see you smiling much?"

"I'm just 'contemplating,' Rose."

" . . . Where did you learn that word?"

"In my dictionary . . . 'Contemplation—noun—to gaze at or think about intently.' "

"That's nice— Keep doing contemplation . . . But I don't like you acting so quiet."

"Sorry, Rose, I was just rememberin' somethin'."

"What?"

"When I was a kid I useta go fishin' with my brothers an' once I caught a little fish an' Lenny made me throw it back because it was against the law to catch baby whales ... Lenny useta be funny— Yeah, he's not funny since he's come back from the army."

Victor's mood was turning gray and he sat limp at the edge of the pier.

"Vickie, let's go dancing tonight."

" ... Ya know I can't dance."

"Then you can watch me."

"Can ya really dance?"

"I won a dance contest once."

"I won a contest too!"

"What'd you ever win a contest for?"

Victor cupped his hand around his mouth and took in a deep breath and exploded with a belch that might have been heard on the other side of the Hudson River.

"That's disgusting!!"

"Wanna hear it again?"

"Alright— Just aim it over there."

18

LENNY SAT IN A BOOTH AT MICKEY'S BAR. He was all alone except for a glass of scotch in his hand.

Business was good and Lenny was just barely able to hear Glenn Miller's "Moonlight Serenade" straining through the bartender's radio.

The more Lenny drank, the more the mass of humanity crowded together in Mickey's barroom resembled a flowing bush being swayed by some stale wind. The leaves on this bush were faces; fat faces, skinny faces, faces that belonged on vegetables, pretty faces with no place to primp. The one face that caught Lenny's interest was a face framed by tangled blonde hair. The blonde flirted with a pair of stevedores and somebody must have told a joke because she laughed and swiveled around, and Lenny saw her face full for the first time. She was really quite beautiful, much too sharp to be doing time in this toilet.

Lenny watched her eye a few men at the surrounding tables and the way she looked them up and down was professional.

She smiled at Lenny.

She easily cast off the bar and glided towards Lenny. Lenny was not the kind of man who smiled easily, but there was something about the temperature, the air, the taste of the booze, his frame of mind, and the sight of the broad that made his mouth curl up.

The blonde knew she was quality by Hell's Kitchen's standards and stood loosely in front of Lenny.

"I'm not payin for it, Vonny."

"You don't even know the price."

"I couldn't afford it if I did."

Four men stood at the end of the bar making a lot of racket. The man with the biggest mouth was missing an arm.

He said, "Hell, if I had to do it over again, I would—I would— Lemme tell you guys something. I ain't no less a man—I'm more of one! Losin' an arm ain't no big deal— No G.I. can't say he weren't proud!"

One Arm took down a double shot of cheap Irish and caught sight of Lenny.

"Hey Lenny."

"Hey, Milt," Lenny answered back.

"Lenny was a soldier too!"

"Yeah."

"He's damn proud too— Ain't ya?! Had his knee blown off day before peace was declared— Don't hear him complainin'."

"I ain't proud, Milt," Lenny said quietly.

"We served— That means something."

"Don't mean I'm proud."

"We both lost a piece over there!"

Lenny could not stand the eyes on him anymore and smashed his cane down on the table and stood.

" ... I'm not proud."

"You are, goddamnit!"

"Of what? Together we don't make a whole man," Lenny said quietly and limped out of the joint.

Cosmo looked at the five young punks then glanced over the side of the roof and watched people going about their business five stories below.

Cosmo spit and started to sink into a racing stance. He looked at the oldest punk with the bumps on his face, "Get this right— Ten roofs, no stoppin'."

"We know the rules," answered a small racer and dropped into a racing stance.

"Then start the race!" Cosmo said and tensed.

The lumpy punk raised his arm, "Ready, set, go!"

Both Cosmo and the Racer pumped their arms and sprinted to the edge of the roof and leaped. Cosmo heard the hollow sound of the alley below, then felt a wave of relief when his feet made contact with the next roof ... The racer had a smoother landing and started to pull away. Cosmo cursed and pumped harder.

Over the second, the third, the fourth, the fifth— He was losing but felt strong. The second half was always his best.

The sixth,

The seventh,

The eighth,

The ninth,

By the time they headed into the tenth Cosmo was close enough to wipe his nose on the racer's neck.

"Run, punk, run!" Cosmo yelled to the weakened racer, "Ya ain't gonna—gonna make it!"

The exhausted racer summoned all his strength to vault the brick chasm, but the muscles in his legs went on strike and refused to do any more, and the racer felt his legs pumping through air, and they continued to pump until his falling momentum angled him through a third story apartment window and into the lives of an elderly couple listening to their radio.

Cosmo hit the finish line and took many deep breaths ... He did not bother to see if the racer was hurt, he just removed the five dollar prize money from under a brick laying on the finish line and lifted his leg over the side of the roof and disappeared down the fire escape.

The tangled wad of dance tickets hung out of Cosmo's pocket as he whirled through the red lights at Sticky's Ballroom. He felt the heat of Annie in his arms and to him there was no better warmth to be had anywhere.

" ... What they need is some fans in here so's you can breathe."

"I'm use to it."

"I don't want ya gettin' use to it."

Annie smiled and eyed Cosmo's ugly, black, baggy funeral suit.

"Where'd you get the suit?"

"Like it?"

"You want the truth?"

"Always."

"It looks like somebody died in it."

" ... Close." Cosmo said, and grinned and guided Annie past a familiar face staring out of the red shadows. Lenny saw Annie catch his eye then he turned on his cane and was gone.

19

MAYBE I BETTER GO IN AN' CHECK THE
place out before ya go in," Cosmo said, and rolled
Annie's door knob in his hands.

"The only things in there are rats," Annie said, and
leaned wearily against the door.

"I'll bring some traps tomorrow."

"Sure—need some sleep, Cosmo?"

"Sure," Cosmo answered, and looked up and down the
black hallway. "Listen, ya gotta get outta this dump—
think about that club act."

"Cos'—maybe we shouldn't be doin' this."

"What?"

"Spending so much time together."

"It's alright—I ain't ashamed of ya."

" . . . Ya know what I mean."

" . . . If ya don't want me around, say it."

Annie looked into Cosmo's proud eyes and lightly
kissed his cheek and closed the door.

Cosmo sure liked this tomato and stared at the door thinking about knocking and forcing his way into her apartment and maybe her heart ... Forget it.

Cosmo put the dreaming away and rocked his weight down the staircase and outside, never seeing Lenny standing across the street, leaning in the shadows.

20

THE SUNSET HOTEL WAS A LANDMARK TO every guy who ever felt three, four, or five dollars could bury his loneliness for an evening. Even though it was nothing more than a shabby whorehouse, in many ways it was as important to the balance of Hell's Kitchen as the Church.

Cosmo moved into the whorehouse and skipped over the huge hole in the carpet that had caused him to trip, oh, maybe a million times.

He moved past the pitted walls and headed toward the beast with old curly blonde hair, propped on a stool behind the reception desk.

"Where's Bunchie this evenin'?" Cosmo asked the beast.

"She's here, Cos'," the madam answered.

"What room?"

" ... Three— Five bucks first— Y'know the routine."

"Listen, Fran," Cosmo said in a friendly way and eyed the goon sitting next to her. "I'll give ya four bucks an' this."

Cosmo fished out an old wrist watch from his back pocket and laid it on the desk.

The beast inspected it and held it to her ear.

" ... Go," the beast said.

Cosmo pried off his socks and stared at Bunchie, the prostitute, propped in bed reading a cheap pulp ... Bunchie was young, but had old eyes and something that had drawn Cosmo to her bed for nearly three years.

"Bunchie?"

"I'm here, Cos'."

"So what bothers me is I keep gettin' the freeze from this tomato. I'm a nice guy—I think so, but I can't get nowhere."

"What do you want me to say?"

"How 'bout two or three words that are gonna change my life."

"Forget her."

"Them ain't the right words."

"Forget her—I'm here."

"Not now, Bunchie."

"I'm the one ya been seein' for three years."

"Ya gotta lotta miles on ya, Bunch."

"Ya not so new either."

"What I need to get in good with her is money."

Bunchie sighed and swallowed her anger. She dropped the magazine and flipped off the covers.

"The clock's runnin'," she said.

21

T

HE FOLLOWING AFTERNOON, VICTOR WAS
driving his dripping truck back to the depot when he saw
a familiar figure in a baggy black suit standing behind a
broken-down pushcart covered with tomatoes.

Victor waved at Cosmo and steered the truck to the
opposite curb, just missing a head-on collision with a
truck full of chickens.

"Whatta ya doin', Cosmo?"

"Expandin'!"

Victor reached out of the truck and squeezed a
tomato.

"Keep ya hooks off the produce! They're delicate—
How would you like it?" Cosmo said, and squeezed
Victor's face.

Cosmo saw three ladies passing down the other side of
the street and he screamed at them.

"Tomatoes here! Fresh off the boat! Tomatoes here!"

"Why're ya yellin'?" Victor said, and looked
embarrassed.

"A businessman has got to advertise, right? Why don't ya go have an accident an' let me expand in peace."

Cosmo stepped back and tipped his hat to a passing cop.

"Get this truck movin', or I'll write you up," the copper said and tapped the fender with his nightstick.

Victor nodded and the man in blue swayed away. Victor again reached down and squeezed a tomato, and Cosmo angrily slapped his hand.

"Do that again an' I'll put your dong in a wringer!"

"I like tomatoes!"

"Ya got enough dirt in ya ears to grow one— So keep ya hands offa mine."

"Sure thing— Whatta ya doin' here, Cos'?"

"This mornin' I gotta stroke of the genius— I drug myself down to the produce market an' swapped that bum monkey to 'Joey Fruits' for the cart an' tomatoes."

"Why?"

" 'Cause a man in love needs fast money— By this afternoon, I'll be in the green— Have a tomato!"

Cosmo tossed Victor a tomato and shoved his cart towards a pair of ladies carrying a basket full of laundry.

"Beauties, I got tomatoes! Big, fat, sassy, happy tomatoes! Listen to them laughing!" Cosmo sang.

The con-man turned and winked at Victor, and the iceman watched his brother and was proud to have a relative as clever as Cosmo was.

"I won't see ya tonight—" Cosmo turned and yelled. "I'm draggin' Lenny to Paradise Alley— He needs some air— Tomatoes here! Happy vegetables."

Victor nodded and bit into the tomato and the warm vegetable exploded and wet seeds slid down the front of his undershirt.

22

COSMO AND LENNY TURNED INTO AN alley on Eleventh Avenue. It was dark, and even together they did not feel safe.

"What're we doin' at Paradise Alley?" Lenny asked.

"C'mon, live a little— Paradise Alley is a great joint."

"I don't feel like 'livin' a little.'"

"They got dames crawlin' outta the woodwork."

"It's a private club."

"No problem."

Lenny was not sure what Cosmo meant in saying "no problem." At the end of the alley, Cosmo knocked on a metal door three times and a big face peered out.

Cosmo looked into the doorman's dead mug and smiled. "We're friends of Mario," he said with flair.

The doorman's eyes swung back and forth between the brothers then he stood aside and the Carboni boys entered into a new world.

"Who's Mario?" Lenny asked softly.

"I dunno— But everybody knows somebody named Mario, right?"

Cosmo turned from Lenny and began to survey Paradise Alley from the top step of the club. Looking down on all the neighborhood's big spenders gave him a great sense of having entered the guarded world of the winners of life.

Even though the place was swollen with smoke, Cosmo could see a brass-railed bar in one corner and in the other corner he saw a four-piece band that blared out catchy music. Cosmo snapped his fingers and elbowed Lenny.

Lenny's eyes were on the opposite side of the room where three crap tables were surrounded by gamblers and women with very white arms and red lips. In the center of the joint, Lenny saw two fighters battling around a small ring.

The brothers crossed to the bar.

"Two beers, Bub," Cosmo said to the squat bartender.

The bartender was annoyed at being called "Bub" by someone as strange looking as Cosmo. He delivered a pair of beers and Cosmo tossed a quarter on the bar.

"It's a buck a brew, Bub," the bartender said tightly and eyed Cosmo's hair.

Cosmo flicked Lenny's elbow and nodded his head towards the bartender, "Get a load of this wit— Since when is dishwater a buck, Bub?"

"Blood or beer, Bub?"

Lenny saw the bartender wrapping his hand around a mallet and fished out a pair of dollar bills and placed them on the mahogany.

"You're a very lucky guy," Cosmo said to the bartender. Cosmo himself never would have given the slob another cent. And if the bartender decided to make trouble, he had a battle plan just dying to be used. He'd wait until "Bub" swung at him, then he would leap over the bar and grab a pair of pretzel dishes and smash them on the sides of the bartender's head. Then he would snag the bartender by his neck and ram his head into the beer pump until the bartender's knees buckled.

What he'd like to do next was great. He wanted to insert his thumbs deep into the bartender's ears, pick him up over his head like Victor had done to Pigpen, and heave him across the club and have the slob impale himself on the roulette spinner, and he would croak while spinning and spinning and spinning, spinning, spinning . . .

The brothers crossed the clubroom and stood next to the boxing ring just in time to see a thick colored fighter named Big Glory flatten his opponent by smashing the man to the canvas and diving on him.

"Did somebody lose a nightmare?" Cosmo said, and studied Big Glory.

Big Glory was on the tall side, and must have weighed near three-hundred pounds.

Dark hair curled across his midnight-black back and
angled down the front of his chest.

Both his arms and shoulders were a fresco of fading
scars.

The eyebrows were gone and Big Glory's ears looked
like a matching set of raw oysters.

The Paradise Alley Club fight manager slipped
through the ropes and raised Big Glory's hand.

" ... The offer of one hundred dollars still stands to
anyone who can stay in the ring three rounds with our
own Paradise Alley champ, 'Big Glory'!"

Maybe one or two people applauded, but it did not
make any difference to Big Glory. The fighter flipped on
a rope and perched his weight on a stool beside the ring.
Big Glory had taped a cigar box to the side of the stool,
which he used for a shelf. On this shelf was a half mug of
beer, a smoldering cigar, and a match stick. Big Glory
puffed on the cigar and, raising a half mug of flat beer to
his lips, looked like a man whose brain was a permanent
resident in another world.

"Hell, if I wuz a coupla inches taller, I'd square off
with that ape myself," Cosmo said.

"I thought you said there'd be some women here?"

"They're probably in the bathroom—"

"What about all the women, Cosmo?"

"They must've died— Whatta ya think about Victor
scufflin' with that ape?"

"Cosmo, the man's a professional, understand?—He
makes his livin' breakin' bones, understand? Why do you

want to turn a professional bone-breaker loose on your brother?"

Lenny did not wait for an answer and limped back to the bar. He did not see Cosmo finish his beer and take a long gander at Big Glory whistling to himself.

23

ROSE AND A GROUP OF NEIGHBORS SAT ON
the steps watching Victor playing stickball beneath the
street lights with a cluster of local urchins. Victor swung
and missed and the children laughed at him.

He laughed back.

On his last try, Victor connected and sent the ball
humming past the kids and even past a group of winos
holding up the side of a building on the corner.

"Vic! C'mon! Lenny's in trouble!!!" Cosmo yelled as he
turned the corner.

Cosmo did not have to say why Lenny was in trouble.
Victor just dropped the bat and sprinted down the street,
past the winos, and around the corner.

Victor suddenly stopped his feet and swung back

around the corner again and looked at Rose standing near home plate.

"Take care of Bella, Rose— I'll be right back!" Victor yelled and disappeared.

24

LENNY? YA SAID LENNY WAS IN TROUble?" Victor said and looked around Paradise Alley.

"There's nothin' wrong, Cosmo just made a mistake—Go home, Victor," Lenny said.

Cosmo was having trouble hearing the dialogue between his brothers in the noisy club, so he edged past Victor and stood in front of Lenny and pointed towards the ring.

"There's a hundred bucks to be had, an' all ya gotta do iz tussle for three stinkin' rounds."

"He's not a wrestler."

"Hey, Lenny, how do you know? Ya gotta crystal ball? It's easy money, Vic."

"What if I getta chipped tooth?"

"I'll cover it with a blanket."

Victor studied Cosmo's expression for a few heartbeats and felt a nervous kick in his stomach. He didn't know if it was the noise, the lights, or the position of the moon, or what, but tonight, Cosmo looked very hungry. The club was dim and because of that it was almost impossible to see into most people's eyes, but not Cosmo's. His eyelids were open wide and the whites framed his pupils and the dark spots burned out of Cosmo's face.

Victor moved towards the door and Cosmo grabbed his arm.

"Always mumblin' about leaving Hell's Kitchen an' buying a friggin' houseboat in Jersey! It's swell ya a dreamer 'cause ya ain't never leavin' this slumbox unless ya wise up! ... You an' that girlfriend of yours ain't never gonna pry your flat asses off the stoop unless ya take a chance, now! ... A hundred clams for a couple a minutes work—think about it, Bright Boy!"

Victor was thinking about it. Thinking so hard that the muscles between his eyes began to ache. A hundred dollars!

"Should I do it, Lenny?"

" ... It's your bones, Vic."

The club's fight manager was slouched against the bar and shooting the breeze with a few comrades. Whenever he said something even half-way funny, his fellow lushes guffawed and the manager would grin and shift his cigar to the opposite corner of his mouth.

Cosmo led Victor by the arm and they wove their way through the crowd and Lenny trailed a short distance behind, his face glowering with disapproval.

Cosmo cracked his knuckles and shifted his shoulders and tried to look as serious as possible.

He tugged at the manager's elbow.

"Okay. Here we are."

"Here's who?" the manager said, and shifted his cigar.

"The athlete who's gonna stay three rounds wid Big Glory."

Victor felt shy and remained in the background, so the fight manager did not see him and instead figured Cosmo was the fool who planned on challenging Big Glory. The manager's face cracked into a half-moon smile and exposed a set of teeth that resembled the cross section of a rotten apricot.

"Him," Cosmo said, and jerked his thumb over his shoulder.

The manager eyed Victor and figured the young man had good size. Maybe he couldn't wrestle worth a damn, but he had damn good size, damn it.

The manager marched across the club and arrived at the ring, followed by his buddies. Climbing through the ropes, he yelled at Big Glory to get ready to kill.

Lowering a mug of beer, Big Glory wiped the foam away from his heavy lips with the back of his wrist, stood, yawned, stretched, shrugged off his fraying robe, and exposed his thick and worn body.

"Okay, champ, ya all set," Cosmo said and rubbed Victor's neck.

Victor felt stupid standing in front of so many strangers in just his trousers and sagging suspenders. All Victor could do was stare at Big Glory's faded scars.

The manager hitched up his pants and waddled to the center of the ring.

"Ladies an' Gents, tonight we're gonna have another idiot challenger who's gonna try an' stay a big three rounds with our own club champion, Big Glory!"

Most of the ringsiders were poor suckers who had already blown their wad at the crap table and now were drunk, and angry, and only a few wanted to place their hands together for a near dead round of applause.

"Now in this corner we have the challenger— What the hell is your name, Kid?"

"Kid Salami!" Cosmo yelled from outside the ropes.

"What's that again, Mouth?" the manager laughed.

"That slob's really gettin' my goat ... His name's Kid Salami!"

"In this corner—believe it or not—is Kid Salami," the manager said then faced Big Glory.

"And in the far corner—the roughest thing in Hell's Kitchen—Smashin', Crashin', Bashin', Big Glory!"

The manager and Glory moved to the center of the ring.

Victor had to be pushed by Cosmo.

"Okay, you guys try fightin' fair."

The manager grinned at Cosmo, exposing his decayed teeth again.

"Where d'ya want the pieces sent?" the manager asked.

"Cut the gabbin', Fatman, an' start the war."

The manager and his big fighter moved away, and Cosmo turned to Victor.

" ... Vic, everythin's gonna be just peachy."

"How do ya know?"

"Would I be smilin?" Cosmo said, and scratched his neck.

Looking down, Cosmo noticed that Victor's legs were shaking and for some reason it struck him funny, then serious. All the while, Lenny simply leaned on his cane and watched, saying nothing.

The manager motioned to Big Glory to murder the kid, then yanked the bell cord and the brawl was on.

Big Glory flowed out of his corner and drifted toward Victor like a growing brown wave of meat and scars; Victor wanted to climb out of the ring and hide in his ice truck. Trying to piece this situation together, Victor stood dumbly in the center of the ring. He tensed his body and prepared to defend himself against the oncoming wave. Big Glory studied Kid Salami standing like a lump in the middle of the ring, then grabbed Victor's face and pulled into a headlock, then smacked his forehead with an open palm.

Victor was dreaming.

Victor was reeling.

Victor's dreaming and reeling came to an end when he fell through the ropes and landed in the spectators' section.

His brothers rushed over to him and pulled him off the lap of a screaming drunk.

"Y'know, there ain't no law against fightin' back, Vic." Cosmo said.

"How bad are ya hurt?" Lenny said, and lifted Victor's head.

Victor was mute and a thin stream of blood drained from a wound above his brow and dripped off his chin.

"C'mon, don't just sit there with ya mouth half cocked— Say somethin'!" Cosmo yelled.

Victor could not speak.

All Victor could do was feel.

He dabbed the wound over his eye and stared for a long moment at the red liquid.

"Better getta doctor," Lenny said.

"We better getta straight jacket ya mean. He looks nutty."

" ... I'm okay."

"Vic, we're goin' home."

"No, I'm all right ... "

"Yeah, let's go home, Vic," Cosmo said and tried to stand his brother up.

" ... No!"

Lenny looked into Victor's eyes and knew his brother was sincere.

"What do you want to do?"

" ... Win."

"Okay, Vic, then win," Lenny said.

No one was sure what had happened, all anyone knew was that Victor had sprung to his feet and leaped into the ring.

He had become a hellcat.

He tore into Big Glory with flailing arms and had the drunk crowd on its feet in amazement. Big Glory did not expect this crazy attack and attemped to shield his face.

But it was too late. Big Glory was hurt, bad, by an elbow smash. Angry youth had caught up to the man.

Nearly all the action in Paradise Alley stopped and the place to turn your eyes was to the tiny ring.

Big Glory began to reel across the canvas square as Victor swung him around in a painful headlock. Big Glory's legs were losing their starch and he nearly buckled in half. Using all his strength, Victor drove his head into Big Glory's stomach and the club champion rocked into an upright position and tumbled over like a butchered hog.

Victor stood panting over the unconscious wrestler and Cosmo jumped into the ring and threw Victor's hand high into the air. He was hysterical.

"Ya great, Vic! Kid Salami! Kid Salami!"

Victor pulled his hand away from Cosmo and moved across the ring and kneeled next to Glory. Victor looked sorry for what he had done and was about to lift the wrestler's head off the canvas when Lenny came over and tapped him with his cane.

"Come on, let's go, Victor."

Victor stayed down on one knee until he was snapped out of this daydream by the sight of droplets of blood swinging from his chin onto Big Glory's chest.

Victor stood up and followed Lenny out of the ring.

The fight manager did not bother to go over to Big Glory because he had figured the bum was on borrowed time before, and now he knew it. Instead, he tapped Cosmo on the Shoulder.

"This Salami Kid ain't a regular kinda guy— He ain't normal ... Wanna sell him?"

"Ya owe us a hundred bucks."

"What about Salami— He for sale?"

"My brother ain't for sale."

25

AFTER THE BRAWL AT PARADISE ALLEY, Victor walked home and stayed mostly in the shadows, because he did not want any of the locals to see the wound above his eye and start asking questions. He was not in the mood for words.

He arrived at Rose's apartment and ran up the three flights and knocked on the peeling brown door until it opened.

Rose was about to say something, but was stopped by the cut and blueness over her boyfriend's eye.

"What happened?"

"I was looking at the moon an'—"

"Yes?"

"An' this bird hit a chimney."

"Chimney?"

"Yeah, an' this brick fell on my face."

Rose's mother heard voices at the front door and leaned her face out of the kitchen.

"Who is it, Rosa?"

"It's Victor ... A brick fell on his face."

Before Rose and her mother could say anymore, Victor reached into his pants and held out the prize money.

" ... I won it."

26

OUR LIL' BROTHER JUST WHIPPED the Paradise Alley champ an' went home with a hundred bucks! Can ya get over it?" Cosmo said while scanning the occupants of Mickey's Bar and rolling a beer glass between his palms.

"He could've got hurt," Lenny said.

"C'mon, he mopped the floor with that gorilla. Remember how I'm always tellin' Vic to find a gimmick? Well, the kid's beef iz a God-given gimmick."

"Don't do it, Cosmo."

"Do wa?"

" ... Just don't do it."

"Ya think I'm gonna try an' push Vic into wrestlin'?"

"That's right."

"So whatta ya got against makin' an honest buck?"

"Depends on how it's made."

"Listen, he don't have to be no pro."

"He don't have to be anythin' except what he is."

"Hey, Frankie's a club wrestler!"

"Frankie's rotten by nature, Vic ain't."

"He can learn."

"Don't try to make our brother into one of your gimmicks!"

"You make me amazed! Here's a one-way ticket outta this slumbox— Where's ya guts?"

"I've got guts, but I've got heart."

"Hey, poke under my ribs and you'll find a heart, too!"

Lenny stared into Cosmo's face and wanted to ram it to the back of his brother's skull, but instead levered himself to his feet. But before Lenny moved away, a hand grabbed his arm and spun him around.

Lenny's face turned blood red and he raised his cane over his brother's head.

Cosmo sneered and spit.

"C'mon, hit me, 'cause ya won't even make a dent. Ya the biggest joke in the whole neighborhood! Ya had brains, you wuz tough, you wuz goin' places, then ya got nervy and joined the Army, an' whatta ya got to show for servin' Uncle Sam? Huh?! A foot locker! A crummy Kraut bayonet! A purple heart an' a friggin' walkin cane! ... Put it all together an' whatta ya got—A first class nothin' with a bum leg! Ya coulda jumped offa chair an' got flat feet like me—Ya coulda stayed here—But ya had to be a hero! How much do heroes get paid?! ... "

Lenny rarely ever listened to his brother, but tonight the words cut and made him weak. His mind felt light and his eyes could not match the stares of the eavesdropping guzzlers.

Cosmo watched his brother disappear out the door and

wiped away the saliva from the corner of his mouth and faced the crowd.

"That useta be the best man in Hell's Kitchen! If ya don't believe it, I'll kick ya brains in!—Well, everybody betta getta good look at Cosmo Carboni now, 'cause I'm on my way uptown— Anybody got a smoke?"

27

LENNY WAS STILL BREATHING HARD when he entered the funeral parlor ... He eyed the dismal surroundings and shoved over a pine coffin.

Lenny cursed at something that was running through his mind and limped to the cabinet, flung open the door and pulled out a bottle of whiskey.

Lenny looked almost hungry the way he swilled the booze and stared with red eyes at a row of cheap empty coffins.

The coffins moved. Lenny was sure they moved! And he was sure he saw bodies! Rotting bodies! Dressed in shredded Nazi uniforms ...

Lenny heaved the bottle at the spectres and limped out of the room.

28

ANNIE WAS LEANING AGAINST THE WALL smoking when Lenny came through the door. She felt her legs stiffen and she watched him side stepping the dancers, making his way to her.

"Stay there!" Annie said and backed away. But Lenny kept coming. " ... Why're you coming around me?"

" ... I want to—I have to."

"Look, leave me be."

" ... I'm sorry, Annie."

Annie tried to angle past Lenny and hide in the ladies room. Lenny grabbed her arm.

" ... Let's talk."

"Now you want to talk—a year I've been waitin' to hear, now I don't want to listen."

"Let's talk."

"No!"

Some of the dancers stopped to hear the growing storm.

"I want to say I'm sorry, Annie."

"You can't make it all better by sayin' you're sorry—
you put me through enough, Lenny— Forget the 'sorries,'
alright?"

"No! It's not alright ... I've had problems."

"Lenny, not in front of these people."

"I don't care— If they wanna listen, good, but I'm
talkin' just to you—ya can see I don't walk so good."

"And you think that would change anything?"

"I'm the one talkin' here."

"So am I!—Did you think I'd feel sorry for you?"
Annie said, and was unable to keep from screaming, "Ah,
I'm so mad I could tear your eyes out! You've been
avoidin' me for a year. No letters, no calls, nothing,
because you didn't want anybody feelin' sorry for you—I
don't feel sorry for you, I feel sorry for me— You did
what you wanted, I'm the one who got left behind."

"I'm back—you want me back?"

" ... No," Annie said softly.

"We were gonna get—"

"No more."

"You can't forget what we had."

"I forgot—now go away."

Lenny had said everything he could and now the
silence was crushing down on him ... He turned and
limped from the dance floor and was nearly out the door
when he heard Annie's voice.

"Lenny—wait ..." Annie said, and came slowly to him.

Cosmo was the last guy left in Mickey's Bar and Big

Mickey was trying to ease him out with hints. Finally the bartender laid it on the line.

"We closin' down, Cos'—get out," Mickey said, and took his glass.

"Sure—ya need the sleep—But I got things to do."

"How's that?"

"Gonna pay a visit to the best skirt in the 'Kitchen,' " Cosmo said, and stood up. "Hey, the glasses were kinda dirty tonight—shape up, okay."

29

COSMO TIPPED THE REMAINING DROPS OF whiskey from the flask on his tongue, then slipped it into his coat pocket, and craned his head up towards Annie's second-story window.

Normally, Cosmo standing on the street would look like any other guy standing on a corner, but Cosmo standing alone this night, covered by darkness, made the man almost look poetic.

He turned the knob on the front door of the building. It was locked. He walked back down the steps and was about to yell for Annie, but, surprisingly, a flash of class made him realize the late hour and he clammed up.

Plotting for a moment, he walked into the tenement's alley and found what he was looking for.

A trashcan.

Hoisting the trashcan by its handles, he carried it out of the alley and set it under the fire escape and began to climb.

The iron work of the fire escape was slippery and

Cosmo almost fell, but managed to swing up to the next level, and in a moment stood breathing heavily outside Annie's window.

The room was dark and in his mind, he had already figured how to play this woman. He would knock on the window and Annie would float from the blackness, wave him in, and they would kiss then crush each other with a hug, etc.

The moon was full and Cosmo could have sworn he saw two bodies lying in bed.

... Goddamn— Goddamn— Goddamn— Goddamn.

Many knots formed in his throat.

... Oh, Goddamn.

Cosmo wiped his eyes and looked harder.

A stick that was leaning against the bed made him swallow. The harder he looked, the more the stick resembled a cane.

In just a few seconds, Cosmo's face aged and he lowered himself to the street. He had to do something with his hands. Heaving the trashcan against the wall, Cosmo walked away crying ... Goddamn— Goddamn— Goddamn ...

30

I DIDN'T EXPECT IT," COSMO SAID, and shifted to a more comfortable position in Bunchie's arms.

"You shoulda expected it—it's his old girl," the young whore said.

"He dumped her— He knew we had somethin' going— He shoulda never let me lead myself on."

"She wasn't your type—I told you before."

"Don't tell me—layin' here in the Sunset Hotel you know everythin'—Is that what ya sayin', Bunch?— Whatta you know?"

" ... I know you."

"They shoulda never led me on."

31

IT WAS EIGHT IN THE MORNING AND
Annie's face was a portrait of sensual exhaustion.

Annie had coffee almost to her lips when she heard a
knock at the bedroom window.

Her heart began to speed up. She entered her bedroom
and even though the sunlight was blasting through the
window and creating a blinding tunnel of hot yellow, she
could see the hazy outline of Cosmo sitting on the fire
escape.

"What happened?" Cosmo asked as Annie opened the
window.

" ... I fell asleep. Cosmo, you shouldn't keep climbin'
the fire escape—it looks bad."

"What do I care, huh?"

"What's the matter?"

"What do you think, huh?"

"Maybe we ought to talk later."

Annie tried to close the window, but Cosmo jammed
his hand beneath the window and flipped it back up.

"Stick around."

"You're hurtin' my arm."

"I oughtta break it."

"What?!"

"I thought we had something goin'."

"We did."

"Yeah, what?"

"We were friends."

"We were more!"

"To you— To me, friends."

"You were just usin' me to keep close to Lenny."

"That's not true! Look, we've got no papers on each other— I'm back with Lenny, because I should be."

Cosmo heard two windows above him open and a skinny man looked out of one and a woman with a face like a boil leaned out of the other.

Cosmo ignored them and dug a cigarette out of his jacket, fired it up, and looked hard at Annie.

"Yeah ... I thought we had somethin' goin'—He's a bum who dropped ya— I treated ya nice."

" ... I love him."

"I don't wanna hear that! Nobody loves nobody around here—everybody fakes it!"

"Cosmo, your brother was the first—we go back a long time."

Annie pulled a cigarette out of her bathrobe, but Cosmo snatched it out of her hand and smeared it on the windowsill.

"This guy ain't the same Lenny."

The fat lady with the boil face leaned so far out of the

window that her jugs hung like a lumpy awning. She shook a blunt finger at Cosmo and screamed.

"Why don't you leave the lady alone!"

"Shut ya fat mouth!" Cosmo fumed.

"I'm callin' the cops!"

"I'll break ya face," Cosmo screamed and grabbed a milk bottle off the window sill.

The Boil retreated.

"Look, maybe you better leave."

"Yeah, maybe I oughtta."

Annie closed the window and left the bedroom.

"You don't like me? Fine! I don't like you neither! What the hell am I, a charity case!?! Ya gonna find out who the better man wuz! Who the hell needs ya! I don't need nobody!"

Cosmo leaned over at the gawking spectators who craned their necks up from the street to watch the free show.

Cosmo spit on them.

"That's right ya maggots, I ain't no charity case!!!"

Taking his shredded pride, Cosmo lowered himself to the street and walked away.

32

LATER THAT MORNING COSMO WAS striding alongside Victor as they headed towards the ice house.

Every few steps, Cosmo would glance down to watch Victor kick a tin can that, when kicked in the right spot, would reflect the morning's rays and glitter down the street. His brother had started kicking the can nearly eleven blocks back, which must have been a Hell's Kitchen record for the longest a piece of garbage had been kicked.

"I know what you mean, honest," Victor said and kicked the can with the side of his foot.

"Vic, last night wuz the beginnin' of somethin' big."

"How big?" Victor said, and kicked the can again.

"I'll be honest with ya— Last night ya fell into the gimmick of a lifetime!"

"Ya really think so?"

"Vic, ya stepped through them ropes a regular iceman an' come out the Paradise Alley champ."

"I didn't feel like no champ."

"Don't worry 'bout what ya feel like, just make me ya handler an' we'll really fill our pockets with somethin' besides lint."

"I can't do it."

"Why not?"

"I promised Rose."

"Ya don't have to promise that meatbag anything!"

"Watch what ya mouth is sayin'."

"Yeah, sure—"

"You should have seen her when she found out— She started cryin' an' her mother yelled."

"So ya got yaself a shiner, I hurt myself worse takin' a shower! Look, ya gotta learn to take and receive."

Cosmo looked down the block and saw the shape of the ice house coming into focus, and got a scratching feeling down his spine. He went over to Victor, put his hand on his chest and kicked the can to the other side of the street.

"Stop kickin' that stinkin' can! I'm conductin' business, understand?!"

Victor swung his eyes from Cosmo and stared at the can as though he had just lost control of a hobby he was beginning to master. He walked across the street and, setting the can in the desired position, resumed kicking it to the ice house.

"Vic, you an' Rosie got plans about gettin' outta this city an' buyin' a— What wuz it ya wanted to buy again?"

"A houseboat in New Jersey."

"Yeah—in Jersey. Well, wrestlin' could be ya passport outta 'The Kitchen' real soon— It's a growin' sport, I tell ya."

" ... How soon?"

"C'mon— Ya want the exact time?"

"I just wanna know when."

"Mebbe two years."

"Can't."

"Why the hell not?"

"I promised Rose."

"Rose's a broad and broads don't know nothin' 'bout fightin'! D'ya know how many guys coulda been squattin' on top of the world, but they let a dame tell 'em what to do an' the only thing these poor suckers ended up squattin' on wuz a toilet!"

"I don't want her cryin' no more."

"You're causin' me to breathe heavy, Vic— Ya got no reason to treat me so crummy."

"Hey, Cosmo, ya know I ain't treatin' ya crummy."

"How long ya been an iceman?"

"You know."

"Yeah, but I wanna hear you say it."

"Since I was twelve."

Victor stopped kicking the can and put it on the windowsill of an abandoned warehouse.

"Whatta ya doin' with that can?"

"I'm gonna kick it on my way home."

Cosmo scratched the side of his face and sighed. If there was one thing he hated in this world, it was the smell of eggs on a dame's breath.

The second was not communicating.

He draped his arm over Victor's shoulder and spoke in a voice that was much too soft to be coming from Cosmo's mouth.

"Victor?"

"Yeah?"

"There's no bones in ice cream."

" ... What's that mean?"

"It means don't be wastin' ya time lookin' for somethin' that ain't there—there ain't no future in haulin' ice, but there iz in fightin'."

Cosmo squeezed Victor's shoulder and grabbed the iceman's chest.

"Brother, this beef iz a God-given gimmick ... Whatta ya say, Champ? We partners?"

Victor looked at Cosmo.

Victor looked at his beef.

Victor looked at his dog.

Victor looked at Cosmo's eyes and thought his brother had aged.

" ... There ain't no grapes in tuna," Victor said.

" ... What does that mean?"

"I dunno."

"Wait, don't go in there—get the truck first—"

"Why?"

"I wanna show ya what real money you can make!"

33

VICTOR GUIDED THE RATTLING MACHINE away from the depot and steered straight to Paradise Alley.

He veered the truck to the curb and, patting his dog, he and Cosmo got out and walked down the littered alley.

Before Cosmo could knock on the door, a man with a thick neck peered out.

"Can we see Glory?"

The doorman stepped aside and let the iceman and the con-man enter.

Even though it was afternoon, the club was still gorged with smoke from the night before and some incurables were still gambling. Cosmo turned his eyes from three musicians who were nodding among themselves on the bandstand, and approached the bartender.

"Is Glory in?"

"Say, ain't you the guy that flattened Glory?"

Victor nodded and the bartender jerked a beefy thumb to the corner of the room.

"Over there— Through the door downstairs."

The brothers followed the thumb and moved down the steps that groaned beneath their weight.

"Forget the layout— It's probably a front," Cosmo suggested.

At the far end of the room he saw a thin cord suspending a tiny bulb. Beneath the bulb was something that looked like a man. They moved closer and were sure the man was Big Glory sleeping on a cot propped across a pair of crates.

" . . . Big Glory?" Cosmo asked.

Big Glory stirred, and after making some sounds that came from his stomach, he opened his eyes.

"Who iz it? Whatta ya doin' here?!" Big Glory said in a voice that sounded like it came from very far away.

"Can I talk with ya?"

"Down here, I don't like yas comin' down here."

"Listen, I'm sorry about what happened."

"Why's sorry? Ya beat me on the square."

After Big Glory spoke, he rolled over and faced the wall, but did not shut his eyes. Instead, he stared at the damp cinder blocks inches from his face.

"He was lucky— When ya hit 'im he thought his head came right off, Big Glory," Cosmo said.

"He gotta head like a rock."

"My girlfriend tells me that," Victor said in a shy way.

Big Glory tried not to smile but could not help himself

and rolled over and looked at Victor who was smiling too.

Big Glory laughed.

It was a warm laugh, but a little rusty from lack of use.

"Got's a rock-head, huh?"

"Like a brick," Cosmo offered.

"Like a brick! Ya okay, boy— Whatta ya wanna talk about?"

"My brother here was wonderin' what it's like bein' a club fighter?"

"Ah ... Like any other racket— If ya'll good, pays off, it does."

"Didn't I tell ya," Cosmo said loudly to Victor, "He just don't waste no money on furniture."

Cosmo snatched a look around the boiler room. He was sure he saw a rat dash behind a trash can.

"Is this where ya live?" Victor asked.

"Hey, this place ain't permanent— My manager, he's savin' all my money. He gots me this setup ta cut corners. All I gots ta do iz fight, an' stoke the furnace three times a day when it gets cold.

Victor nodded, but did not want to look around the boiler room. The place made him feel like he had lead in his gut.

Big Glory coughed, scratched his nose, and pointed to a cracked picture of himself tacked on the wall with a three-quarter inch iron bolt.

"That's me when I wuz in good shape."

"Nice picture," Cosmo said.

"Nice, yeah— My manager's savin' my dough, an' when he gots enough, he gonna start my career over again."

"How long's he been savin?" Cosmo asked.

"Ahh ... I ain't sure."

"Probably any day now ... Well, let's get movin', Vic," Cosmo said, and wanted to leave this wasteland without wasting another minute.

"Can I ask ya another question, Big Glory?" Victor asked.

"Sure."

"How old are ya?"

"Forty-one ... Forty-four, but I can still wrestle. Even ya sez that."

"Yeah, ya can still hit," Cosmo said, "Let's blow, Vic."

"An' I'm gonna whack my way up the ranks again— gotta family, ya know."

" ... Yeah?"

"Sure—I gotta beautiful wife an' two boys. One wants ta be a fireman an' the other a radio talker."

"How come ya don't live with ya family?" Victor asked.

"You a detective? With all the dough Glory makes they most likely live grand-like upstate," Cosmo offered.

"Yeah, to get ahead in this racket, ya gots to have sumbody ya trust bein' ya handler—. Ya gotta have sumbody ta trust ... Remember that, Boy," Glory said.

"Remember that, Vic— Well, Big Glory, we gotta go now," Cosmo said and stood.

"Hey, what's ya name?"

"Victor the iceman."

"Listen, Victor the iceman, if either yall boys wanna talk again, I be here, okay?—This iz where I live . . ."

Victor and Cosmo climbed the stairs and paused at the top . . . It felt good leaving Big Glory's troubles down in the basement.

"Don't let that dump throw ya— Wrestlin' is a good career— I see what's comin' in the future— Y'know, a little paint an' some rags an' Glory would have a nice place down there— Look, forget what ya seen."

"It don't look like he's got money," Victor said softly.

"Maybe he blew it at the track, we don't know the story— Whatta ya say?—We partners?"

"I gotta go to work," Victor said, and started to walk away.

"Good, go to work. But I'm laughin' at ya—That's right, laughin'— 'Cause I'm growin' big an' ya gonna stay small, Ice Head!" Cosmo said in one breath and turned to the bartender, "Whatta ya got strong for two-bits?"

34

THAT NIGHT VICTOR LOOKED EXHAUSTED
as his body swelled over the small frame chair in Rose's
kitchen ... He and Rose were eating something large
covered with sauce which now smeared around their
mouths and made them look like a pair of Italian clowns.

"What if I said I wanted to be a wrestler?"

"No."

"Why not?"

"It's bad, Vickie— Eat your dinner before it gets stiff."

Victor's clamps bit into a long block of ice and he
heaved it onto a wood wagon, then started to pull the
wagon out of the ice house. The door opened and he saw
the Polish foreman's face coming slowly into view. The
foreman put his sandwich into the crook of his arm and

pulled out a small brown envelope from his shirt pocket.

Victor counted his meager salary and smiled at the foreman. But,

Victor's eyes no longer,

Smiled.

35

ENNY?"

Lenny turned and saw Victor standing in the doorway of the embalming room. Victor had just come from work and red ice burns were patterned across the top of his arms and shoulders.

"I don't need any ice today, Victor."

"I know— I wanna talk with you, Lenny."

" 'Bout what?"

"Ya gotta minute?"

Lenny smiled at him. If there was one person in this world who had lots of time, it was Lenny.

"I think I can spare a few— Sit down."

"Nah, I wanna walk around— Lenny, I'm gonna be a wrestler."

" ... You're makin' a big mistake."

"That's what Rose says, but I gotta make money to get outta this place."

"You're workin' steady— Take your time— The money will come."

"For three years I been savin' an' all I got is a hundred an' six dollars."

"Is movin' to New Jersey worth gettin' your brains beat out for?"

" ... Yeah, I think it is."

"But you've never been to New Jersey— How d'ya know you'll like it?"

"I just know."

"Look, forget about fightin' an' stick to what you're doin'—"

"There ain't no future in haulin' ice!—My beef iz a God-given gimmick."

"I see you, but I hear Cosmo talking. Come back when you're just Victor.

Victor turned and walked out into the hallway, then walked back in.

"Okay, it's just me this time .... You can be a good handler."

"Go home."

"A real good handler."

"Go home!"

"Lenny, ya gotta!"

"If you wanna get hurt, don't ask me to watch— Get somebody who don't mind watchin' like Cosmo."

"If ya was my manager, I wouldn't have to worry about nobody stealin' my money."

"No!"

"Lenny ... I won't have to carry ice no more, an' you won't have to work here no more— D'ya like workin' here?"

Lenny limped over to the ice boxes and leaned against the silver latch handle.

His leg throbbed.

Lenny let his eyes wander across the room. He had never been proud of his craft. In an instant, he was mad, vexed, harassed, and thoughtful. The balance had been upset.

"Victor, you go out an' think real hard. If you still want to do it, come back an' we'll talk."

36

VICTOR DROVE THROUGH HELL'S KITCHEN
and everywhere he looked was permanent dirt. He looked
at the rows of over-turned trash cans and wondered why
nobody ever picked them up.

He saw a dead cat that someone had kicked into the
street and left there for the flies to eat.

He looked at two mick kids fighting and at a bum
sitting in the gutter trying to find out where he dropped
his future.

He had seen these scenes
Lots of times before, but it
Had never bothered him before.
. . . Today it bothered him.

Victor stopped the ice truck on 47th Street. It was a
hot day and his undershirt stuck to his flesh like gray
wallpaper.

The sweating customers did not wait for Victor to ring the truck-bell, they just leaned from the windows and screamed for service. It was as though they blamed Victor for the heat that tortured them and cursed the iceman for being so slow.

Victor stroked his dog and picked a tick off the animal's ear, then lifted two dripping blocks of ice and walked into the building.

He climbed the first two floors without any problem, but half-way up the third flight, he slipped on an empty wine bottle and fell. The ice scraped against the side of his head and sheared the back of his ears and caused them to bleed.

Victor almost cursed.

He took a deep breath and picked himself up and started to climb again, but his strength was melting like the ice he carried until Victor reached the top landing and stood still.

His whole body trembled.

He tried so hard to think why he should feel this way but he could not hear his thoughts. The only sounds he could hear were from the customers screaming for ice!

Ice!

Ice!

Ice!

For the first time in his life Victor made an important decision. He bucked the ice from his shoulders and watched the blocks avalanche down the stairs and tear pounds of plaster out of the wall.

Victor walked downstairs, stepped outside, and tossed the iron clamps into the truck. He picked up his dog and set her on the ground. The customers leaned from their windows and screamed like prisoners.

The iceman and the dog walked away.

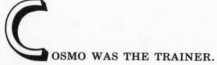OSMO WAS THE TRAINER.

Victor was the fighter.

They stood together in a vacant lot covered by a field of cracked bricks and bent plumbing fixtures that rose out of the rubble like twisted metal weeds.

Cosmo stood with a cigarette jammed in the corner of his mouth watching his brother throwing bricks as far as he could.

"C'mon, heave them rocks!"

"How long do I have to do this?"

"Listen, I'm the trainer an' I'm tellin' ya to shut ya trap an' heave them bricks— This iz good exercise to beef up them arms an' shoulders."

"I'm beefy enuff."

"Hey, I'm the one who decides what's beefy enuff— Heave!"

Victor looked at his hands and the blisters that had already been filled with water and split and now the skin looked wrinkled, damp and covered with red brick dust.

They hurt, bad, but he kept throwing anyway.

"Hey, Cosmo, where'd ya learn to be a trainer?"

"It's a gift ya born with— Now throw that radiator."

Victor walked across the rubble and pulled out a rusting radiator, hoisted it over his head and heaved.

Lenny came around the corner and limped across the broken stones.

"Victor, you're all set to fight tonight at the Blue Door Club."

"Thanks, Lenny!"

"You're welcome."

Victor wiped his hands on the front of his shirt and whistled to Bella and started to walk away.

"Wait a minute! Where're ya goin'?" Lenny said.

"To tell Rose the good news."

"You should go home an' rest up."

"Nah, my beef feels strong, right, Cosmo?"

"Look, I don't feel nobody's beef."

Victor did not want to hear any more words and he and his dog walked away.

Lenny was upset and rolled his cane between his fingers and looked at Cosmo smiling.

"Got problems, big man?" Cosmo asked.

"No problems."

"Kinda look down in the mouth."

"I got no problems."

"Takin' this managin' job pretty serious, ain't ya?"

"I didn't ask to be a manager, Victor came to me."

" ... Everything comes to you, Lenny."

"Understand this—Your job is to keep Victor in shape,

my job is handlin' the business, that's it."

"What if I ain't satisfied with this crap-o arrangement?"

"Join the Navy."

Cosmo remained silent and watched Lenny limp away. He could not stop his hand from wrapping around a brick and throwing it. It landed an inch away from Lenny, but Lenny refused to notice it and kept limping away.

"I could kill ya—I could kill ya—ya had to take her back."

" ... Yes."

"Why?!"

"She was mine."

"Ya dumped her— Then ya took her back 'cause ya couldn't stand me havin' her."

"Don't mix in it."

"I don't wanna hear no more— You an' the dumb broad can go to hell— I'm just in it for the money."

"Watch your mouth."

"Whatta ya gonna do about it?

Lenny just limped away.

38

T HE THREE BROTHERS WERE RINGSIDE AT the sleazy Blue Door Club that night.

Outside, another angry summer thunderstorm was raining away on the club's roof. The water found the many holes in the rotting ceiling and snuck in. The true fans ignored the wetness and pulled their coats over their heads while more diehards sat ringside beneath umbrellas— But it was as though the Devil had planned to place the biggest leak above the ring which fauceted a stream of water onto the canvas, until the ring sagged and the fighters were forced to stand ankle deep.

Cosmo helped strip Victor to his shorts and street shoes, while Lenny watched intently as the water dripped from the brim of his hat and onto Victor's shoulder.

Cosmo pulled out a roll of black electrical tape and started to wrap Victor's hands.

"Couldn't ya find any other kind of tape?" Lenny asked.

"What's wrong with electrical tape?" Cosmo snapped.

"Victor's a fighter, not a broken toaster."

Nickels Mahon and his gang sat at ringside beneath a strip of old gray canvas they had found beneath the ring. They looked like a herd of rats beneath the cloth. They smiled and showed their teeth and pointed at Victor.

Mahon's gang put their fingers in their mouths and started to whistle when they saw Irish Patty McLade sway towards the ring.

It was easy to see that Irish Patty McLade was a seasoned battler whose features had been rearranged by leather fists.

Cosmo looked across the ring at Patty McLade and swallowed, then spit to make everyone think he was full of confidence.

"Listen, don't play patty cakes with this turd— Waffle 'im—Waffle the turd."

Cosmo wiped the black residue from the tape on the sides of his pants and stared at the soggy fans, who sat at ringside beneath a folded newspaper. Surrounded by leaks and creeps, these people did not look like they would win the prize for being the most thrilled fans on earth that evening.

Lenny was staring at Victor very hard when the promoter stepped through the ropes and raised a megaphone made out of cardboard with his right hand and covered his head with an umbrella lodged in his left hand. Just before he spoke, thunder and lightning caused the lights to blink on and off.

"Listen up! In this corner, weighin' 255 pounds in his first club fight, Victor Carboni!"

"Kid Salami!" Cosmo yelled.

Nickels Mahon stuck his head out from beneath the canvas and yelled towards Cosmo.

"Kid Greaseball, ya mean!"

"His name's Kid Salami!" Cosmo screamed at the promoter.

" . . . Kid Salami," the promoter said and sighed.

"Die, ya bum!" Nickels yelled.

The Carboni brothers expected to hear some applause, at least three or four pairs of hands beating together.

Nothing.

Instead of applause, they got razzberries from Mahon's gang and Pigpen heaved a tomato that squashed against Victor's knee.

"Die, ya dago punk— Die!" Pigpen yelled.

"Ya mother was a—" Skinny the Hand started to yell.

"No mother stuff," corrected Nickels.

In the far corner, weighin' about 245 pounds—" The announcer tried to say and was interrupted.

"250!" Patty McLade yelled.

"Weighing two hundred an' forty pounds, Irish Patty McLade!"

Mahon's gang roared and stomped their feet and Cosmo almost flipped them the finger, but decided against the move because he did not want it torn from his hand while he was still in the prime of life.

Lenny wiped the water off Victor's face, but it did not do any good, because the iceman was thoroughly drenched. Cosmo bent down and measured the water in the ring with his hand and shook his head in disgust.

"Don't fall down, brother, or ya might drown."

Before Lenny could give any more instructions, the bell rang and the wrestlers were waved to the center of the ring.

Victor sloshed forward and offered to shake Patty McLade's hand.

"Wanna shake first?"

McLade ignored the hand and sent a forearm exploding into Victor's jaw.

Victor was staggered.

The Irish cheat followed through with another blast and blood flowed down Victor's chin.

McLade swung Victor around from every angle trying for the quick kill, but he didn't bank on Victor's oak legs and the iceman remained upright.

The round ended and Cosmo splashed to the center of the ring to help his brother on the stool.

" ... He's strong."

"He's a dirty, cheatin'—"

"My teeth hurt."

"Ya brother's a real bum. Ya bring a box to take him home?" Nickels yelled.

"Maybe we oughtta throw in the towel," Cosmo said to Lenny. "Vic ain't got the heart."

"I come to win," Victor said.

"Forget it, you're startin' to look like a nightmare," Cosmo said and wiped the blood away from his brother's nose.

"I'm okay, honest."

"Ya sure?"

Lenny moved Cosmo aside.

"He said he's good— Okay, Vic, you've come to win— Win!"

The Irish wrestler leaped from his corner before the bell's echo had even died away. From the look in his eyes, it did not take a genius to know that he was primed to put the finishing touches on Victor.

Instead,

Victor lowered his head, closed his eyes and rammed McLade's body with the force of an El train.

McLade tried to hook his thumb in Victor's eye, but the iceman grabbed McLade's arm and swung him into a turnbuckle, and holding him up with his right arm, pounded the Irish bum's body into cream cheese with his thrusting shoulders.

... Patty McLade dropped to the floor like a whore's nightgown.

"!!God Bless America!! That wuz terrific!" Cosmo screamed.

Nickels Mahon's gang could not believe what they saw and left the club without a smile among them.

Lenny snatched a glance at them, then turned and watched Victor splash over to the fallen wrestler and help lift the man out of the water. "Ya okay?"

McLade returned to the land of the living and realizing Victor was sincere, nodded and swayed back to his corner.

Victor was about to leave the ring with his brothers when Cosmo waved him aside and spoke low and fast to Lenny.

"What ya done tonight was wrong," Cosmo said.

"Problems?"

"Yeah, problems— When Vic got hurt, we shoulda quit."

"And start the career off with a loss?" Lenny asked.

"Who cares?"

"I care," Lenny said, and moved past another wrestler climbing into the ring.

Lenny tucked the pillow beneath his neck and stared up at the dark ceiling.

" . . . When Vic was out there—I felt like I was out there."

"Are you sure it's the right job for you— Him being your brother and all."

"Nothin' wrong with winnin'," Lenny said, and embraced Annie. "When the money starts comin' in—"

"I know— We'll get married— You better."

" . . . Depend on it— Let's get some sleep."

39

VICTOR JOGGED AND COSMO PEDDLED THE warped bicycle along the waterfront.

Victor pointed to a deserted pier.

" ... Remember when we was kids an' used to go fishin' over there?"

Cosmo lifted his dull eyes and aimed them at the pier.

"... The river smells."

"That's my favorite place in New York."

Cosmo was about to argue about that fact when he saw Frankie the Thumper and Nickels Mahon's gang heading towards them.

Frankie was pulling a cart and the gang rode in the back and drank beer, and broke the bottles against anything that caught their fancy.

"Mornin' girls, I see ya keepin' ya sister in shape, Cosmo—this iz the way Frankie trains, not like a coupla ugly broads on a bicycle," Nickels said and swilled beer.

Frankie the Thumper set the cart down and stared at Victor.

"Soon, we're gonna meet in the ring, ya punk," Frankie yelled.

"Pull, Frankie—Iceman, ya better be in shape, 'cause when ya meet Frankie, he's gonna rip you apart like ya wuz an old sheet."

"Nickels, I've had a very rough day," Cosmo said and kept moving.

"Couldn't ya find no cigarettes in the gutter?" Nickels said, and the gang laughed.

"Nickels?"

"Yeah?"

"Y'know some people might think ya a bigshot, but me, I think you're a very small asshole."

Frankie the Thumper dropped the cart and rushed Cosmo, but he stepped out of the way and Victor jumped forward and took the blow on his chest. Frankie tried again to maul Cosmo, but Victor surprised him with his speed and swung beneath his ape arms, and shoved the big man off the pier. Cosmo had gotten behind the gang and put his shoulder to the cart and the cart, the gang and two cases of warm beer plunged into the river.

It was almost noon when Lenny walked into the Paradise Alley Club. There were about ten hard-cases still gambling from the night before. It did not matter if it was noon or midnight to them, all that mattered was the feel of the club. To know that they could get a drink when they wanted and hear the sharp clicks of the bone dice when they wanted, and maybe screw a five-dollar hooker in the cloak room, when they wanted.

Paradise Alley may not have been an ideal world, but it was a simple one.

"Who do I talk to about promotin' high-stake fights?" Lenny asked.

The bartender shrugged and rotated a glass on a white cloth then placed it on a mirror shelf.

"I asked a question."

"I just serve the booze, Pal."

A thin gambler with sharp clothes and a bent nose swayed over from a dead crap table and leaned against the bar. The bartender automatically poured a shot and placed it next to the gambler's hand.

"What do you wanna know?" the gambler asked.

"I've got the best club scrapper in the 'Kitchen' an' I'm lookin' for big-stake matches," Lenny said.

"What's the bum's record?"

"Two fights, two wins."

The gambler smiled and spoke to Lenny like he was a child.

"I take it you're a guy without no patience."

"I don't believe in wastin' time," Lenny said.

"Lemme tell you how the club-fight racket works, okay? ... The way ya make big green off ya wrestler is by havin' him build a rep, then you bet on him— That's how you make big dough. But your bum's gotta have a good record before people start bettin' heavy Jack— Now you wanna come back after, say forty or fifty matches. Then you'll be ready to win some important cash. Until then, ya fighter iz strictly small-time."

"We'll win fifty in the next four months—no trouble."

"Listen, if the bum scraps fifty times in four months, he ain't gonna have enough brain left to tie his shoes."

Lenny had gotten the information he had come for and wanted to hear no more from a bent-nosed gambler, whom he thought was no more than a skinny collection of germs stuffed into a suit worth ten times more than the body.

Lenny limped away and the gambler took a racing form out of his pocket and smoothed it on the bar. The gambler clicked his fingers at the bartender, who poured him another shot.

"Y'know, that guy just ain't impatient, he's desperate," the gambler said and flipped the page.

LENNY STOOD VICTOR ON A CRATE ON THE corner of 49th and Seventh and watched the crowd grow around him.

"Friday night at the 'Kitchen Club'
See Kid Salami tear Butcher Bill apart!
Be there— Bring money— Be early, because
It won't be a long one!"

VICTOR FOUGHT IN THE DINGIEST CLUBS in New York City.

He beat Herman the German, Tiger Wilson, Butcher Bill, Benny the Plug, Harry von Brun, and a lot of other scrappers whose names he couldn't even remember. But one thing he did remember was that he had felt sorry for every one of them as he pounded them to the mat.

42

THE MONEY WAS SLAMMED ON MICKEY'S bar and placed on a stack beside another growing pile of green. Lenny was on the telephone behind the bar watching the money stacks grow.

"Sure, I know what time it is—"

"I haven't seen you for three days," Annie's voice came through the receiver.

"I got work to do— Look, Annie, I can't talk now, I'll see ya later."

" . . . Don't waste your time."

"Listen, I'll be by later," Lenny said, and hung up. He picked up his cane and limped around to the front of the bar and spoke in a loud voice.

"Who wants to cover this fifty?! I say my brother will whip 'Kid Coffee' in the first, 'Freddy the Idiot' in the fourth an' next week, pin 'Kid Sullivan' in one— Who wants my action?"

BACK IN THE RING, VICTOR DESTROYED Mack the Stick, Freddy the Idiot, Drafty McDonald, Vincent the Schemer, Rockhead Rozelli, and again, many others he had never even been introduced to.

After the Rockhead Rozelli fight the brothers were seated in a greasy spoon. Lenny watched as Victor tried to down a huge bowl of spaghetti.

"I can't eat no more."

"Gotta keep up ya weight," Lenny offered.

"My head hurts."

"Just a headache—got to cover up more, Vic."

Cosmo eyed Lenny and lit another smoke.

"Yeah," said Cosmo, "Cover up. Lenny don't wanna be wastin' no dough on quack doctors— Right, Len?"

Lenny eyed Cosmo and tapped Victor's shoulder, "Vic, listen, since you're called Kid Salami, I want you to hang a few Salami's around your neck."

"How come?"

"It'll be your trademark— It'll be good for business."

And Lenny was right, because the chant of "Salami—Salami—Salami!" filled every match joint in Hell's Kitchen, and after every victory it was becoming a custom for Lenny to climb into the ring, hold Victor's arm up with one hand and a big salami in the other . . . God, the fans loved it.

44

VICTOR'S MATCHES WERE BECOMING AL-
most routine slaughters.

The only thing different was that Victor's face was
beginning to change shape and Lenny was looking more
like a fashion plate every day.

All this had been driving Cosmo crazy.

He could not understand the bad change in Lenny's
behavior, and for the first time

In his life

Cosmo really wanted to kill his

Brother.

45

COSMO'S FEET SCRAPED ALONG THE WELL-
worn grooves in the stairs climbing to Sticky's Dime-A-
Dance joint. He knew what to expect at the top: smoke,
red lights, laughs, tired music, and Annie.

He saw her dancing with a sailor and waited until the
tune was finished and walked over to her.

" ... No hard feelin's," Annie said first.

"No," Cosmo answered, and pulled out a cigarette, "I
just came up to get a light."

"Here," and the match flared in the con-man's face.

"Thanks ... How's life treatin' ya?"

"Fine."

"Ya better slow him down," Cosmo said flatly, and
left.

It was nearly sunrise when Annie and Lenny paused
on their trek homeward.

"I'm telling ya, I can't spend no more time with ya—I'm workin'."

"So what? We all work— I don't like you acting like this."

"Then maybe we oughtta forget the whole thing," Lenny said, and lit a cigarette.

"Forget?"

"That's what I said."

"Look, Lenny, I don't care why you got into it—I just want you to stop what you're doing."

" ... Look—I'm doin' what I want to be doin', understand ... I got business."

Before Annie could think of anything that might stop Lenny or even slow him down, he was gone around the corner, and the only remaining trace of Lenny was the fading taps of his cane on the sidewalks of Hell's Kitchen.

MICKEY'S WAS CROWDED AND CRAMMED with noise, but it did not bother Lenny and the tall blonde hooker, Vonny, who sat together in a booth.

"I was wondering," Vonny asked, "wondering where you went."

"Keeping busy."

"Your name's getting around."

" ... Everybody needs a name."

"Before you said you couldn't afford me."

Lenny smiled and drained his glass.

"Let's go to your place," Lenny said.

IT WAS THE MIDDLE OF OCTOBER AND Victor was scrapping once every four days. This night he was to do battle with "Rat" Sullivan.

Lenny was limping towards Victor's dressing room, when he passed Rat Sullivan's trainer, who was hauling a basket full of oranges toward the ring. Lenny stopped the trainer and inquired what he was planning to do with such a large supply of fruit.

"I'm takin' them over to cut up for the Rat."

"Why?"

" 'Cause he likes to suck a piece of orange between rounds," the trainer said.

Lenny buffed the top of his silver-headed cane with the cuff of his jacket and grinned.

"Guess the Rat plans on doin' a lot of suckin' tonight," Lenny said and flicked the oranges.

"There's two dozen of 'em here."

Lenny lit a cigarette and tapped the basket of fruit with his cane.

"You wasted your dough, friend."

"What're ya talkin' about?"

"Your boy won't be needin' any oranges tonight— You should've invested in Band-aids instead."

Lenny grinned again and limped away from the trainer and entered Victor's dressing room.

Round One

At the bell, Rat Sullivan grabbed Victor around the neck, slipped behind and seized him in a bear hug. Victor's head snapped back from the sudden jolts by the vise around his chest.

Lenny's face was ice.

Cosmo looked back at his battling brother just in time to see Victor shift, drop low, and send a curling forearm into Sullivan's stomach.

The Rat doubled up and another hook contorted his face.

The Rat fell face forward. Out. The match did not last half a round.

Maybe Rat Sullivan and his trainer would have the oranges for breakfast.

Cosmo had watched Victor very closely during the Rat

Sullivan scrap and was very disturbed by what he saw.

Even as a kid, Cosmo remembered that Victor was the nicest guy in the neighborhood. You could call him "dunce" and it wouldn't matter, or give him a hot-foot, stick gum in his hair, or fart against his leg; Victor would always take it with a smile.

When he became an iceman, Cosmo remembered riding probably a million miles with his brother and recalled how some of the ugly customers would yell at the iceman for being slow and stupid, but Victor never said a bad word.

Cosmo recalled that even during the first thirty matches, Victor had always felt sorry for the man he had just destroyed, but that was changing.

The more Victor fought, the more he seemed to like it and now when he drove a man to the mat, he would yell at him to get up— Not to rise and leave the arena, but to get up for more painin'.

Cosmo flashed back to the Cowboy Jack match, when Victor had split the Cowboy's eye. Victor yelled at Cowboy to keep fightin', and even after the referee had stopped the brawl, Victor still wanted to do battle and challenged anybody in the house.

But Cosmo knew it wasn't Vic's fault that he was changing.

The more Victor would punish the other wrestlers, the more Lenny liked it. Lenny had been drilling it into Victor's head that to be a great fighter that people respected, you had to be a killer.

Victor the iceman was becoming a killer.

After the Rat Sullivan fight, the brothers walked down the short brick corridor towards their dressing room.

Cosmo fished through his pockets until he found a cigarette and jammed it in his mouth. He looked for a match, but could not find one and rather than ask someone for a light, stuck the cigarette back in his pocket.

"I think we ought to talk," Cosmo said and tapped Lenny on the arm.

Lenny turned to Victor and lifted his cane and pointed to the dressing room.

" . . . Shower up," Lenny said.

They saw the door close behind Victor, and Cosmo threw the first words.

"Y'know, this ain't right what ya doin'."

"Somethin' botherin' you, Cosmo?"

"Yeah, Victor needs a rest."

"I take care of business, not you, Cosmo."

"Look, he's winnin' but he's gettin' smacked too much—"

"If ya don't like the sight of blood, you're in the wrong racket."

"Hey, I ain't talkin' 'bout some bum, I'm talkin' about our brother! Ya makin' him crazy!"

Talking time was up. Lenny wiped the top of his silver-headed cane with a handkerchief and limped away.

Cosmo felt the veins in his face stretching the skin tight across his forehead.

"!I dunno this guy?! Who the hell iz this guy?" Cosmo yelled.

The only answer Cosmo heard was the tip of Lenny's cane tapping and echoing down the brick hallway until the echo entered the dressing room.

Lenny crossed the dressing room and tried not to breathe too deeply because the ingrown stench of blood, sweat and waste-decorated walls made him want to gag.

He moved around the first rub-down table and angled towards Victor, who sat in the nook of a shadowy corner. Lenny noticed that in the past few months, Victor's face had become hard and his voice hard, too.

"Well, Vic, tonight ya won your fortieth fight, what've you got to say about that?"

"Disoriented."

"You and that dictionary. You don't sound so happy for a man who's gettin' rich."

"I'm happy, but I don't think Cosmo is."

"Don't worry about him— You just stay healthy."

"My ears ring a little— How much money have we got, Lenny?"

"What d'you want to know for?" Lenny said tightly.

" ... I just wanna."

"You don't trust me, Victor?"

"Sure."

"Faith—do you know what faith means?"

"Yeah."

"What?"

"Faith means believin' in something invisible."

"Then don't mix in business, Victor— I'm doing what's good for you, so have faith," Lenny said, and walked away from his "disoriented" brother.

COSMO PULLED UP HIS COLLAR TO WARD off the invading snow flakes that fell on Christmas Eve. He sipped from a flask and moved down 49th Street past rows of window decorations and colorful ribbon that looked out of place in the "Kitchen," but the Christmas spirit had somehow punctured the dumbness of the neighborhood and was now to be enjoyed by a few inhabitants. Cosmo even had bought presents.

Cosmo swung down Ninth Avenue and past three winos who tried to wish him Merry Christmas and pick his pocket.

Cosmo shoved one of the winos, who fell over his own feet and came to rest in the gutter.

Cosmo swayed past Mickey's Bar and was tempted to go inside, but looking through the diamond square on the front door, he saw Nickels Mahon and his gang and swayed on his way.

Cosmo rounded the corner and saw the Sunset Hotel sign covered in gray snow ... He skipped up the stairs and entered the stink hut.

"Merry Christmas," the madam beast said from behind the registration desk.

"Yeah—I want to spend some long time with Bunchie."

"How long?"

"All night for starters," Cosmo said, and started to pull out his money.

Nickels crushed out his cigarette against his heel and headed for the crapper.

Once inside the stench hole, Nickels fired up another smoke and studied his mug in the spotted mirror. He touched the growing lines around his eyes and greasy creases carved in his forehead. He felt himself becoming angry then dizzy with depression. Christ, another Christmas! He might have even cried if Frankie the Thumper had not stumbled out of the stall, trying to button up his pants.

Frankie's face broke into a huge drunk grin and he looked ten years old.

"Merry Christmas, Nickels!!!"

Sour was the mold of Nickels' face.

Frankie's smile faded and he looked twenty-eight years of age.

"Ain't ya glad I whipped that Big Glory tonight?"

"Sure— Merry Christmas, Frankie."

Victor and Rose spent the night watching a double bill at the Criterion Theatre in Times Square. The first show was "White Christmas" and the other was the first version of "The Christmas Carol." Sitting through both shows, Victor would feel a buzzing in his ears and the words coming from the actor's mouths would get soft and all he could see were lips moving. Then the voices would come back, then fade out again, then in again.

After he and Rose had left the theatre, they window-shopped for twenty minutes, then headed homeward. At first, Rose was trying to make talk about the movies and Victor just nodded his head. Then she started talking about the houseboat, or maybe not houseboat, just boat in New Jersey that they would someday have.

Again, Victor nodded and continued to walk.

Rose could see she was getting nothing but a lot of nothing from Victor and turned the talk to what she thought might be a cute topic.

"What letter are ya up to in your dictionary?"

Victor did not answer and scratched his neck.

"I said, what letter are you up to?"

She could not believe it that Victor could be this rude and she tugged his arm lightly.

"Didn't you hear me?"

"What?"

"I've been talking to you."

"I must be contemplatin' again, 'cause I didn't hear nothin'."

Rose's face tightened and she paused at the steps of her building and studied Victor staring blankly at the falling snow flakes being reflected in a street lamp.

"Do you love me?" Rose said softly.

"What?"

"Vickie, you're not hearin'."

"No, I feel okay."

"You're hurtin', Honey."

"I feel great, honest."

"Listen to me."

"I don't want to argue, Rose."

"You're getting hurt, understand?"

"I'm okay— Let's look at the snow."

"Forget the snow, your hearing is going."

"Let's get somethin' to eat," Victor said, and pulled Rose into a diner.

The hallway was pitch black as Lenny made his way upstairs to Annie's apartment. He knocked and after a moment Annie answered and stared at Lenny silhouetted against the blackness.

"Any love in there for me?" Lenny said smoothly, and pulled a present from behind his back.

" ... I'm surprised you showed," Annie answered dully.

"It's Christmas," Lenny said with flair, and entered. "Let's get the celebration goin' 'cause I've got to leave in an hour."

"Leave where?"

" ... Business."

"On Christmas. Business on Christmas— Lenny."

"I know, but I'm setting up the best matches yet ... Merry Christmas, Ann."

Cosmo looked at Bunchie and thought she looked

younger than ever. She was pretty, and smart for a hooker, but he could never love her. Something was missing. But he sure as hell liked her. Damn, hadn't he spent a fortune visiting her for the past three years ... Close to four hundred bucks he would guess.

"Since when did you become a giver?" Bunchie asked and fumbled with the wrappings on a small package.

"Just open."

"It's beautiful!" she exploded, and held the pearl necklace high in the air.

"From across the room they'll look real."

Bunchie smiled and started to open the second present.

"Ya oughtta see my brother's face."

"Why?"

" 'Cause it's a mess."

"Maybe he ought to quit— What's this?"

"A stopwatch."

"Plan on settin' a new record?"

"I was," Cosmo said, and got to his feet, "Look, I gotta go out for a while ... "

49

Cosmo carefully moved down the steps and stood in Big Glory's basement. He heard the steam pipe banging and above that, Christmas music crackling from a small radio. Cosmo looked around the boiler and saw the radio propped on a crate beside Big Glory's cot.

"Big Glory?"

"Whatta ya say?" Big Glory said, and raised his head and watched Cosmo cross the boiler room. "Ya name is Cosmo ain't it?"

"Yeah—I just come over to see how ya was doin'."

Now that he was closer, Cosmo could see that Big Glory had just taken a bad fist beating and his face resembled twenty pounds of blue meat.

"Look at my mug an' ya can see I ain't doin' too good."

"What happened?"

"I had a fight wid this bum named Frankie."

"I know Frankie."

"Dat bum, stay clear of, he bad weather."

"Why're ya scrappin' on Christmas?"

"I do what I'm told— Been hearin' a lotta good things 'bout ya brother, Salami—comin' up fast."

"He's been scrappin' a lot."

" . . . He wuz a good lookin' kid once."

"Sure ain't no more."

"I bet he ain't!" Big Glory said, and laughed. "Yeah, we both sure ain't no bathin' beauties, huh?!"

Big Glory gave out a horse laugh then shifted his weight to his left elbow and rolled to the other side of the cot and plucked a cracked photograph of himself that he had impaled on the wall.

Big Glory stared at the picture then held it up to Cosmo.

"I never was no bathin' beauty."

"Ya want some wine?" Cosmo asked.

" . . . I'm thirsty."

"Whatta ya say we both go out an' have some fun tonight?"

50

LENNY LIT A MATCH TO MAKE SURE THE staircase was clear, then started down.

"I know you're mad, but some things just work out this way."

"Do they?" Annie said, and leaned against the railing.

"Yeah."

"What color hair does this business meeting have?" Annie said with a tight pain in her throat.

"What're you sayin'?"

" ... I'm sayin' maybe you shoulda never come back here."

" ... Maybe you're right," Lenny said, and continued down the staircase.

"You bastard!"

"Maybe we're not the same people anymore, Ann—I'm

tryin' to be the best at something, but you're holdin' me back."

"Just like that—it's over."

" ... Yeah, just like that," Lenny said, and was gone.

51

COSMO AND BIG GLORY GRABBED THE OLD chain and yanked.

It snapped like a rotten shoelace.

They walked into the ice house parking lot and moved past a row of new trucks until Cosmo stopped in front of his brother's old machine and got behind the wheel.

Big Glory looked at the newer ice trucks and frowned.

"Hey, Cos', they got sum nice ice trucks here. How come the junk you choose?"

" 'Cause she's the only one I know how to start."

Big Glory pulled his frayed coat tighter around his thick body and got inside the truck.

Christ, what drove out of the parking lot sounded more like a giant tin can suffering a nervous breakdown than a truck, but the noisy thing still managed to work and Cosmo wheeled the bastard down the street and around the corner.

Cosmo steered the truck through the sleeping neighborhood and approached a group of slumping winos and rang the bell. The pack of winos nearly trampled each other to death trying to get out of the truck's way as it bumped over the curb and swung down 47th Street heading towards the river.

"Lemme drive—I ain't drived in years— Lemme drive!"

Cosmo did not try to stop the truck, instead, he let go of the steering wheel and got out of the seat. The truck was steering itself as Big Glory sucked in his belly and slid behind the wheel.

Cosmo rung the bell and Big Glory drove like a crazy man.

Just for laughs, Big Glory wheeled the truck on the sidewalk and chased a pair of winos while weaving between telephone poles.

"Ice! Ice! Ice!" Cosmo and Big Glory yelled.

Ringing the bell with all his might, Cosmo laughed and Big Glory steered the machine down the sidewalk, while yanking over trashcans.

The neighborhood was now wide awake and people leaned from their windows and screamed until it looked like their stomachs were going to jump out of their mouths.

Bottles and flower pots smashed on the hood of the truck, causing deep dents in the rusty metal. At first, the noise shocked Big Glory and Cosmo, but when they realized they were not in danger beneath the canopy, they laughed louder.

"Ice! Ice! Ice! Santa Claus iz here!" Big Glory screamed.

The more Big Glory drove, the younger he looked. He looked like a punk kid when he steered the truck up to Mickey's Bar and stopped in front of two sailors who were trying to latch on to a tired hooker.

"Hey, why didn't ya come home last night? The kids waz cryin' an' everythin'," Big Glory said.

"An' Grandma fell outta the window!" Cosmo said, and laughed.

The sailors did not have to look long at Big Glory's mangled face before they felt scared.

"That ya ol' man?" the sailor said to the hooker.

Before the hooker could focus on what the hell was happening, Big Glory pulled down his pants and roared like a big lion.

" ... RRROOOAAAAAAAAARRR!!"

The sailors spun on their heels and broke into a run and Big Glory shrugged at the hooker and squeezed her cheek.

"Sorry, Toots, but us lions gotta roar now an' then."

Big Glory and Cosmo laughed as hard as two men could laugh and the truck rattled around the corner and disappeared into the dark.

Big Glory and Cosmo dangled their feet over the side of the deserted pier and swung their legs in the breeze that blew off the river.

"Cos ... Y'know, I gotta hand it to ya, I ain't had such a ball since I don't know."

"Me neither, Big Glory."

"Hey, ya don't have ta call me Big Glory no more."

"How come?"

" 'Cause I ain't so big, just fat."

"Fat Glory ain't such a catchy name."

"It ain't catchy, but it's closer ta home ... Y'know, before we went hell raisin', I wuz thinkin' a lot ... Y'know, a big deal I ain't no more."

"Don't be sayin' that, Big Glory."

"Hey, I ain't Big Glory."

" ... Fat Glory."

"Cos', I ain't no big deal no more."

"Ya shouldn't bad-talk yaself."

"I ain't bad talkin'—I been thinkin' 'bout this for a long time. I finally figgered out I'm livin' backwards, ya understand? All them things that made me feel good, they happened a long time ago ... Ya understand what I'm sayin', Cos'?"

"But ya manager's gettin' ya ready for a come-back."

"That guy weren't no manager, he just worked there ..."

"What about all the money you won?"

"For the last ten years, I been wrestlin' just for room an' board ... So before I go, I just wanna say thanks for bein' a buddy."

"Where're ya goin'?"

"I'm gonna jump in the river."

"Why?"

" 'Cause I feels good."

"I don't get ya."

"Most people bump themselves off 'cause they's feelin' pretty blue. Now, when I feels blue myself, I don't feels like hurtin', I feels like hurtin' somebody else."

"I still don't follow."

"I always wanted to end it when I felt good—Tonight I feels good."

"C'mon, I'll take you home."

"Hey, remember this—"

"What?"

"Nobody in the world has gotta do nuthin' if they don't wanna."

"Whatta bout ya family?"

" ... I ain't got no family. That wuz just a story I made up in my head," Big Glory said, and smiled.

Big Glory stood up, but Cosmo felt weak and just sat trying to think of something smart to say.

"Let's drive the truck some more."

"Nah, I made up my mind, but thanks for bein' a buddy— Now gimme ya word ya won't try no hero bit— Gimme ya word."

Cosmo suddenly leaped up and grabbed Big Glory.

"No, I ain't gonna give you my word! I ain't givin' nuthin'!! Ya tryin' to make me feel bad 'cause my brother was the one who started ya down."

Calmly was the way Big Glory peeled Cosmo's hands off his jacket.

"Hey, Cos', ya brother didn't beat me, I din't want it no more— I'm happy, don't spoil it," Glory said in a soft way.

Big Glory reached into his pocket and pulled out the

folded picture of himself and handed it over to Cosmo.

"Look hard at dat an' do some smart thinkin'."

The big scrapper shook Cosmo's hand and lightly smacked his cheek, then stepped to the edge of the pier.

Glory turned and waved, and the con-man tried not to, but waved back.

"Don't worry, 'cause in a hundred years this iz gonna matter none!" Big Glory said, and jumped.

The fighter's black body made a loud splash when it hit the black water, then soon there was a black quiet. Cosmo was not sure if this had really happened or he was dreaming and this was at the tail end of some nightmare.

Cosmo knew the answer to that question when he looked down at the cracked photo of Big Glory that hung in his hand.

52

THE FOLLOWING MORNING LENNY SAT ON the edge of Victor's bed, smoking and looking very important compared to Victor, who had buried half his face in the pillow.

"Alright—you want to call it a day—is that right, Vic?"

"I'm just gettin' sore more— I don't like it no more," Victor said, and tried to bury more of his large head in the pillow.

"Alright, if ya wanna quit, I won't be mad. But I thought you were made of harder stuff—I did think that, Vic," Lenny said calmly, and flicked his ash.

"Whatta ya mean?"

"Harder, you know—gutsier."

"I got guts."

"Sure ya do, but how much?—Listen, Vic, I think you're the best."

"Thank you."

"You're welcome— An' I'm just a little disappointed 'cause the big money was just startin' to come in."

"How big?"

"Very big— Maybe even a thousand dollar purse."

" ... Who do I have to wrestle," Victor said, and started to pull his face out of the pillow.

"I don't know if you have the stuff."

" ... Who?"

"Forget it— If ya get hurt I don't want ya cryin' to me that I put you up to it."

"I don't cry—who?"

"Frankie the Thumper."

"Frankie?"

"Maybe you're not ready, Vic," Lenny baited.

Before Lenny could finish his thought, the door opened and Cosmo came in looking and feeling dead ... He swayed to his bed and layed down.

"Hi, Cosmo—I beat him in arm wrestlin'."

"I can't afford to lose money if you're scared, Vic," Lenny said, and lit another smoke.

"I wanna fight—if you don't, I'll set it up myself," Vic said, and sat upright in bed.

"Alright, you convinced me— I'll set it up, Vic."

"Who?" Cosmo said, and rolled over to face Victor. "Set what up?"

" ... Frankie."

"You can't do that," Cosmo said hoarsely, and put his feet on the floor. "Frankie'll murder you."

"I beat him in arm wrestlin'."

"Vic, don't say dumb things—there ain't no comparison between the two—Frankie's a hurter."

"Victor's undefeated," Lenny offered, and stood up.

Cosmo ignored the words from Lenny and pleaded with Victor.

"Vic, ya ain't in no shape—ya been pushed too hard," Cosmo stopped speaking and grabbed Lenny. "Set it up, I'll get ya, ya greedy bastard!"

"I'm gettin' sick of ya threatenin'— He wants it not me," Lenny said, and pulled away.

Cosmo shoved Lenny and Lenny raised his cane to crack Cosmo's skull—Victor grabbed the falling cane and looked into Cosmo's eyes.

"Don't fight, Cos'."

Cosmo pulled himself free and tightened his jaw muscles . . . "Go get the money."

"I'll see you later, Vic," Lenny said, and left as though nothing had happened.

Cosmo paced the length of the basement, absently flicking out at objects until he faced Victor from the other end of the room.

"Ya poor bastard—Ya don't know nothin'— Look at ya face."

"I don't have to look in the mirror."

"Do you know where ya headin'?" Cosmo asked.

" . . . On a houseboat."

Cosmo could not listen to any more and angled past Victor and moved out onto the street.

53

PIGPEN SHOVED TWO TABLES TOGETHER
and it looked like every guy who was a true sportsman in
Hell's Kitchen was gathered at Mickey's that afternoon.

Nickels Mahon and his gang sat on one side of the
table and Lenny and Victor bordered the other half.

"We're here to talk business, so let's talk— Whatta ya
guys wager?"

"Make ya bet," Lenny said.

"You first, Carboni."

" . . . A hundred."

"Peanuts— Bet money, I can't buy nuthin' with peanuts."

Victor leaned over to Lenny and cupped his hands
around his big brother's ear.

"How much money we got?" Victor whispered.

"What d'you want to know for?"

"I just wanna."

"Nine thousand an—"

Before Lenny could finish, Victor wheeled around to Nickels.

"We wager nine thousand!" Victor yelled.

To say that Lenny went white ...

"Sounds like a hefty wager," Nickels said and winked to his gang.

"For nine grand, I'll tear his face off," Frankie the Thumper said.

"Yeah, that's a very healthy wager, kid," Nickels said, and winked at his gang.

"I want to discuss somethin' with my broker," Lenny said and walked to the other end of the room with Victor.

"What the hell did you do?" Lenny snapped.

"Whatta ya mean?"

"Ya just bet everythin' we own!"

"Me an' Rose want to get the houseboat soon."

"Forget Jersey! People like us don't live in houseboats."

The words hit home and Victor was very hurt and stared for a long time at Lenny's inflamed expression.

"Victor, if ya lose this fight, we're finished, we're garbage again, understand?"

"I was never garbage, Lenny."

" ... Can you win for sure?"

"Yeah."

"How can you be so sure?"

" 'Cause ya have faith."

Lenny studied his brother's plain expression and returned to the bargaining table.

"When do you want to set the fight?"
"Tonight," Nickels said matter-of-factly.
"Short notice."
"You yellow?"
" ... Tonight it is."

54

CHRIST! PARADISE ALLEY WAS PACKED TO
the rafters. Gamblers were going nuts trying to lay bets
in every corner of the room, but no matter how loud
they yelled, someone was yelling louder.

It was very difficult to conduct business and the
bartender was hog-sweating trying to serve the customers that lined up three deep at the bar and bellowed like
a sea of mouths.

The main battles were for the seats. Soon as one
sucker got up, his seat was swiped and immediately sold
to the highest bidder.

The whole neighborhood was there. Everywhere you
looked there was a familiar mug. The bartender from
Mickey's, Mr. Chinzano, the barber, all the tomatoes
from Sticky's, Patty McLade, the wrestler. Nobody was
a stranger to Paradise Alley that night.

Outside, a good show was starting. People shoved and
smacked each other to get in, but if God himself had

lowered a giant shoehorn from Heaven, Paradise Alley could not have another body pried into it.

Little children who should have been in bed were curled on the sidewalk and pressing their faces against the window to get a view of the ring.

The Carboni brothers were in the dressing room and Cosmo was busy taping Victor's wrists as Lenny buffed the head of his cane and nervously paced in front of the rubdown table.

"You're gonna win tonight, aren't you?" Lenny asked.

"I'm gonna win."

"Ya better, Vic," Lenny said firmly.

"Don't you believe?" Victor asked.

"Just make sure you win."

"He's fightin'—get off his back," Cosmo said, and wiped away the sweat from his forehead and fired up a cigarette. He looked at Victor gently stroking his dog and was about to give a few words of encouragement when he heard Lenny's voice again.

"Sure, I believe in ya. Just win, nothin' else counts, understand?"

Cosmo had been waiting for this confrontation for at least the past four years, and now here it was, and over what?

"Y'know, you oughtta take that cane an' shove it in ya ear, 'cause ya brains crippled worse than your leg could ever be!" Cosmo yelled.

" ... Later," Lenny said in a dry, threatening voice.

"No 'later'—How about now?" Cosmo challenged.

" . . . Later, Cosmo."

Victor watched the way Lenny and Cosmo were looking at each other and he felt very sick deep in his stomach. He might have gotten even sicker if the Paradise Alley fight manager had not stuck his head in.

"Alright, ya guys are on deck," the promoter said, and disappeared.

Cosmo helped Victor into a jacket made of small salami's strung together and all the brothers left in silence.

Moving down the hallway leading to the ring, Victor felt the noise building in his head. He looked at Lenny walking up ahead and turned to Cosmo who was carrying the stool and bucket.

"Lotta people here," Victor said.

" . . . You can back out."

" . . . You don't want me to back out— Ya oughtta be proud."

"Why ya say that," Cosmo asked.

" 'Cause it was you who started everything, Cosmo."

Lenny stopped at the entrance and yelled back at his brothers, "C'mon, let's move, Vic!"

Victor and Cosmo looked across the ring at Nickels Mahon rubbing Frankie the Thumper's neck and Cosmo thought that Frankie looked so mean that he could win the fight just on his rotten appearance.

Frankie spit at the Carboni brothers and shook his fist.

"First I'm gonna smash you! Then I'm gonna get you!

I'm gonna kick ya head to the river! I'm gonna tear ya mouth off!"

Rose sat at ringside and applauded Victor even though Victor had done nothing worthy of applause, so far, and a thin smile stretched across his face when he saw her blow a kiss.

"Keep covered, watch your eyes, keep covered," Lenny instructed.

"Everythin's good, Lenny."

"Ladies an' gentlemen, tonight this bout will have no time limit. The rounds will go 'til one of these guys falls!" the ancient ring announcer proclaimed.

"Listen, I din't start nuthin'" Cosmo whispered to Victor.

" ... Yeah, ya did, Cosmo." Victor answered, and stretched.

A roar went up and more bets were placed.

"In this corner, weighing two hundred and ninety-six pounds, with a record of one hundred seventy-four wins, and nine disqualifications— One of the greatest wrestlers in the history of Hell's Kitchen—Frankie the Thumper!"

More than half the crowd was favoring Frankie and gave the big man a wild cheer.

A pair of drunks jumped on the apron of the ring and patted Frankie on the back, and Frankie shoved them to the floor, and Nickels took a couple of wild kicks at their heads.

"In this corner, weighing two hundred and sixty-two pounds, with a record of forty-one straight wins, a guy who got his start right here, Victor 'Kid Salami' Carboni!"

"Vic, ya can take a powder if ya want— You don't have to fight, Vic— We'll work something out with Mahon," said Cosmo.

" . . . Na, I'm doin' it for myself."

"Win, Vic," Lenny turned and said mechanically.

"Watch his thumbs."

" . . . Sure— See ya later," Victor said, and made the sign of the cross.

The first round opened with Victor rushing from his corner and reaching out with both hands, grabbing Frankie by the neck. The strategy was simple and good because he slipped behind the giant and seized him in a powerful arm lock then switched to a hammerlock and shoved the bum through the ropes and had him hanging off the apron of the ring.

The crowd could have been a flesh volcano the way they erupted, and spewed out more bets and cheers.

Frankie was crazy-mad when he climbed back into the ring and wasted no time and nearly broke Victor's neck with a vicious flying leg kick. Frankie the Thumper had meted out some of his best twisting tortures and Victor took them gladly, and stood toe to toe swapping forearm smashes with the mountain for the final two minutes of the round.

The bell rang and more cheers went up.

Frankie the Thumper had surrendered his brain to the world of kill and ignored the bell, and pounced on Victor, when the iceman turned his back. They fell to the mat and it took the men from both corners and the referee to separate the tangled ball of muscle.

"Get this animal off my brother!" Cosmo yelled.

Nickels Mahon led Frankie back to his corner and threw water in the fighter's face.

"I'm gonna kill him. I'm gonna kill him," Frankie said.

"Good, Frankie, good," answered Nickels.

Lenny was telling Victor how to move and to slow down and save his strength when the bell for the second round rang.

"Everythin' is fine, Lenny— I'm enjoyin' myself," Vic said.

"Don't enjoy— Get mad— Win!"

Frankie rushed out of his corner and attacked Victor before he was even off his stool. The Thumper landed a knee drive into Victor's gut then bashed him with a forearm high on the chest that nearly drove Victor's heart through his back.

Victor countered with a twisting arm lock that shook the big man with pain.

Cosmo yelled that there were only ten seconds remaining in the round and Victor dropped low and bulled against Frankie's tree thighs and again Frankie nearly sailed through the ropes when the bell rang.

Frankie spit in Victor's face.

"I'm gonna kill you," Frankie said, and stomped back to his corner.

"Kill, Frankie, kill," encouraged Nickels.

Victor returned to his corner and smiled. "Frankie's 'abnormal.'"

"Sit down, Vic," yelled Cosmo.

"Don't get careless! Win, Vic!" Lenny yelled.

Round three was a gem and the crowd knew.

Victor and Frankie fought like evil dogs with Frankie's body slamming Victor then switching to grinding headlocks and wrist chops that swelled Victor's ears to twice their size.

Victor recoiled then came back with a flying scissor kick on Frankie's chest that nearly cracked the man's breastbone.

Cosmo's chewing his thumbnail caused blood to seep from the quick as he watched his brother pounding and getting pounded.

Frankie dragged a pair of wrist rubs across Victor's face and shoved Victor against the ropes by clubbing him with his elbow. Victor bounced off the ropes and gripped the long hair under Frankie's arms and dropped to the mat. Frankie bellowed in pain and screamed something dirty in Italian.

The bell rang and both men returned to their corners.

As soon as Victor sat down, Cosmo was quick to apply ice to his brother's raw eyelids.

Lenny leaned through the ropes and whispered in Victor's ear.

"You're doin' great, Vic, but ease off, ease off and pick your holds."

"Ya mean 'discriminate' my holds, Lenny."

Cosmo removed the ice from Victor's face and stared angrily at Lenny.

"Like what ya see?"

"Why don't you dry up! You got him into it!"

"Don't fight," Victor said in a soft voice.

The bell rang and it took no prodding to have the men lunge at each other.

Both scrappers were desperate and bore inside each other with terrible body blows. Anybody sitting in the audience knew that these men would be on their backs for a month.

They stumbled,

They slipped,

They lumbered,

And kept up a crushing attack until the milling in the center of the ring had become a blur.

It was near the end of the round that Victor saw the best opportunity of the evening, and he caught Frankie around the waist, and shipped him halfway across the ring with a hip roll. Frankie landed face down. He crawled to his feet and elbowed Victor with the force of a jackhammer.

In the corner, Lenny and Cosmo were frantically attending to Victor who now was floating on dream street. He listened to his brothers' words, but that evening he was not in the mood for instructions, and merely shook his head to try to make like he understood everything Lenny was saying.

"You're winning, Vic, you're winning," Lenny said.

" . . . Substantial."

"What did he say?" yelled Cosmo.

"Encroach," Victor said idly.

"What're you sayin', Victor?" asked Lenny.

"What round is it?" asked Victor.

"Christ! He don't even know what round it is," Cosmo said and looked pleadingly at Lenny.

Before Lenny could tell him he had had enough, the bell rang and Victor charged Frankie.

Frankie focused himself on the charging iceman, set his body, and put all of his weight behind a donkey kick to the jaw.

Victor was floored.

The crowd became crazed; Rose cried.

In those first few seconds that Victor lay sprawled, he thought about how dying must have felt laying there, beaten, the crowd turning vicious and wanting to see you dead, not caring that a vicious beating could leave you a breathing potato for the rest of your life.

Victor scanned the ringside faces and they all seemed to belong to one angry person.

Victor staggered to his feet and moved out of the way just as Frankie rushed past.

Victor felt his head clearing and stepped to the center of the ring, waving Frankie to come forward. The men stood toe to toe, straining back and forth in a double arm lock for the remainder of the round. By the time the bell rang, the crowd had become so crazed that several fist fights erupted in the stands.

In Frankie's corner, Pigpen and Skinny the Hand attended to Frankie, as Nickels leered across the ring at Victor. Nickels pulled his jacket aside and fingered the white grip of a cheap .32 revolver tucked in his waistband.

"If he don't drop soon, I'll drop him."

"We gotta stop this," Cosmo said.

"You stop nothin'! We got nine grand on the fight! How ya doin' Vic?"

"What round is it?" Victor said.

Again, the bell rang and Victor instinctively rushed from his corner, deaf to his brother's words to quit.

Frankie drove into the iceman with a vengeance, but Victor was not to be outdone and met Frankie's fury head-on.

Victor crowded in close and tried to use the strength that had made him famous in the neighborhood, but both men were worn, and if an edge had to go to either, odds had Frankie.

Frankie saw a perfect opportunity and he charged Victor and grabbed him in a bear hug, then shoved his face against the turn-buckle. Backing away, Frankie got in the perfect choke hold that caused Victor's eyes to become bulging glass, then the Thumper turned him around and unleashed hell on Victor, and Victor, again, dropped.

This time, Victor had no thoughts running through his mind, and staggered to his feet. But Frankie had Victor's number and drove his heel between Victor's eyes and the iceman dropped again.

Cosmo wiped the tears away with the side of his sleeve and screamed for his brother to stay down. The only one screaming louder for him to stay down was Rose. But Victor heard nothing but a tuneful wind that was blowing through his head and out his eyes and back in his ears again. It was a soothing song that lulled him into a trance and he had to fight very hard to keep from lying down and enjoying the music of pain.

Victor groped to the ropes and hauled himself to his feet. But Frankie was his shadow and spun the iceman around and with all his strength sent a lethal skull butt into the iceman's forehead.

Victor was out.

The crowd screamed and spectators tried to rush into the ring ... And Lenny just stared at the audience with disbelief.

"He won't come around— We gotta get him up!" Cosmo yelled.

"Get him up— Vickie!" Rose yelled.

Before they had a chance to sit Victor in an upright position, Nickels, Frankie, and the rest of the gang swayed across the ring and stared down at Victor like he was nothing more than a stain on the canvas carpet.

"I hope the Carboni bums know that the better man won. The stiff tried, but he wuz just outclassed— Let's have the dough, greaseball."

"Get away," Cosmo said tightly.

"What'd you say?"

Cosmo took an envelope out of Lenny's pocket and flung it in Nickels' face.

"I said for you to get away," Cosmo threatened, and shoved Nickels to the floor.

" ... Frankie!" Nickels yelled.

Frankie grabbed Cosmo around the neck and started

to maul him. Cosmo tried to drive his thumbs into the gorilla's eyes but he was overpowered.

The spectators stopped paying off bets and crowded around the ring once again to watch the second Carboni brother get destroyed.

No one believed what happened next. How could anyone have figured Victor would jump to his feet and seize Frankie and whip him into a turn-buckle. Victor functioned like a mindless battering ram. The crowd watched the big man sag to the canvas, a broken heap of flesh. And Victor hoisted him to his shoulders and heaved him to the second row.

Nickels got scared and drew his pistol and aimed at Victor. But as he fired, Cosmo snatched Lenny's cane and brought it down on Nickels' hand and knocked the pistol to the canvas, then swung the cane in a whistling arc and broke the black shaft across Nickels' face.

Cosmo lunged at Skinny the Hand and threw him down on the canvas, kicked him in the jaw and rolled him out of the ring with his foot. Pigpen started to run for his life, but he did not run fast enough and Cosmo shattered a bucket against the back of his head.

"Victor, what happened. Weren't ya knocked out?" Lenny said in disbelief.

" ... No," Victor answered, and hugged Rose.

"You threw the fight?—Ya threw the fight?! Ya blew everythin'!"

" ... Yeah."

"Why? Why the hell ya do it?"

" 'Cause I liked it better when we was just brothers ... "

Lenny grabbed Victor's arm and reddened. "What the hell does that mean?!"

Cosmo pulled Lenny around to face him and smacked him on the jaw and watched Lenny stagger into the ropes.

" ... Wanna know what it means?—It means he loves ya," Cosmo said, and backed away.

Lenny's vision cleared and he watched his people departing and for the first time since the war he felt very alone.

"Hey, Vic— Vic!" Lenny beckoned.

Cosmo and Victor stopped and looked at the oldest brother propping himself up against the ropes.

"Could ya give me a hand— Somebody broke my cane," Lenny said.

EPILOGUE

IT WAS NOT LONG AFTER THE FIGHT THAT Lenny had pawned most of his jewelry and sat in a small neighborhood Italian restaurant. Lenny poured his date a glass of homemade dago red wine and watched her sip the ruby liquid. "How's the wine?" Lenny asked. " . . . Delicious," Annie answered and smiled.

Victor veered the ice truck to the curb and hauled two blocks into Mr. Schwartz' shop.

Mrs. Schwartz watched Victor with a smile as he walked to the back of the store and shoved the ice in the box like he had done a thousand times before.

Victor wiped his hands and walked up to the counter and Mr. Schwartz feebly threw him a piece of penny candy.

"How come you're not married yet, Victor?"

" 'Cause I ain't rich yet, Mr. Schwartz."

As Victor passed along the counter, Mr. Schwartz held
out a handful of Brazil nuts.

Victor smiled and crushed the nuts, and stepped
outside.

The old man handed the shattered nuts to his little
wife.

"Eat these," Mr. Schwartz said.

Cosmo was on the corner of 46th and Ninth standing
behind a table covered with assorted religious statues
made of plaster. Some of the statues were odd; Jesus' left
arm was missing on one, on another Michael the arch-
angel was missing his head. Cosmo eyed the small crowd
and took a deep breath.

" ... Ya house can't be complete without one— It'll
give the rooms class— It'll give ya somethin' to leave to
ya kids when ya croak ... An' these are one of a kind,
made by some of the best artists in Hell's Kitchen. They
might have a few flaws, but that's why I can afford to let
'em go so cheap."

Cosmo watched Bunchie cross the street holding a
small brown bag.

"How's business," she asked.

"Rotten— What's for lunch?"

"Ham an' cheese— Be by at six?"

"Bank on it— Ain't she beautiful— Bunchie Adams."

Bunchie blushed and looked relieved to move away
from the appraising eyes.

" . . . Yeah, a great broad," Cosmo said, and watched Bunchie disappear around the corner. "Alright, now for what ya been waitin' for— The special of the day!"

Cosmo bent over and pulled out a small crate covered with a cloth. He put the crate on the table and flipped back the cloth and smiled broadly.

"C'mon, what do I hear for this gem? What do I hear for Kid Salami's very rare shorts? Huh? What do I hear for the shoes he wore when he jumped on Frankie the Thumper's face—the laces are separate."

"One dollar for the shorts," somebody yelled.

"Try again— An' here's a real collector's item— Worth a fortune someday!—Hate to let it go— What do I hear for Kid Salami's original meat jacket?!"

"My God, it smells," said a lady in a cheap cotton dress.

"Just varnish it an' ya won't smell nuthin'— Take ya time, think it over— Alright, here I have Kid Salami's toothbrush, almost never used."

"One dollar!"

"Sold!—And what do I hear for a small bag of dog hair belongin' to Salami's great dog, Bella! C'mon, people, my feet are gettin' sore . . . Now what do I hear?—What do I hear?—What do I hear . . . . . ."

THE END